THERE'S A
BAT IN
BUNK FIVE

THERE'S A BAT IN BUNK FIVE

PAULA DANZIGER

Hodder
Children's
Books

a division of Hodder Headline Limited

First published in the USA in 1980 by Delacorte Press.
First published in Great Britain in 1980 by William Heinemann Ltd.
This revised edition published in 2001 by Hodder Children's Books.

The right of Paula Danziger to be identified as the Author of
this Work has been asserted by her in accordance with
the Copyright, Designs and Patents Act 1988.

10 9 8 7 6 5 4 3 2 1

ISBN 0 340 79538 7

Typeset by Avon Dataset Ltd, Bidford-on-Avon, Warks

Printed and bound in Great Britain by
Clays Ltd, St Ives plc

Hodder Children's Books
a division of Hodder Headline Ltd
338 Euston Road
London NW1 3BH

Publisher's Note: It is now illegal, under the Wildlife and Countryside
Act 1981, intentionally to kill, injure or handle without a licence a bat
of any species in Great Britain, or block the entrance to their roosts,
without consulting the Nature Conservancy Council. The events in
this book take place in the United States. In Great Britain, none of the
15 resident species of bat is harmful to people or animals; in fact, as
consumers of vast numbers of insects, bats are a useful friend to man.
Nevertheless, because of various threats to their normal habitats bat
numbers have severely declined, and this has led to them becoming a
protected species.

One

If I iron or sew one more name tag on my stuff, I'm going to scream. There are name tags on my jeans, shorts, shirts, nightgowns, pyjamas, sheets, pillowcases, sleeping bag, socks, sweaters, sweatshirts, underwear, and jackets. My mother's having me put adhesive-tape labels on my comb, brush, and flashlight. There's indelible ink on my fingers from putting my name on my sneakers. She'll probably make me carve my name in the soap bars and on my glasses frames.

'Marcy, can't I help you with anything?' My mother sticks her head into my room.

'No thanks. I can do it myself,' I say for the eighty-millionth time.

She walks in. 'Here. I addressed some envelopes for you with our address on it and put stamps on them. That'll make it easier for you to keep in touch.'

'Look, I promise, I'll write. You didn't have to do that.' Sometimes they act as if I'm three years old, instead of fourteen and eleven twelfths.

She puts the stationery in my suitcase. 'It's the first time you've ever been away for such a long time. I'm going to miss you.'

I continue to iron. I know I'm going to miss her too, but I really want to get away, be on my own. I really want to get out of the house since I'm always kind of tense in it.

She keeps on talking. 'I wish I'd had the chance to go away to camp when I was your age. You're so lucky, being part of a creative arts camp, with Ms Finney as the director.'

I nod. I've thought about little else since I got the letter from Ms Finney asking if I'd like to fill a last-minute vacancy and be a counsellor-in-training, a CIT, at the camp. I've missed her so much. She's the best teacher I ever had, one of the few who really cared about kids. She quit after a big fight with the school administration.

We wrote for a while, but I hadn't heard from her for months. Then one day I came home and there was this letter asking if I'd like to work on the camp newspaper and assist in the creative writing programme. I was in shock, so excited I thought I'd die of joy. Overwhelmed.

My father, however, was underwhelmed. It took a long time to convince him I should go. He's always afraid I'm going to be too radical or something. He hated Ms Finney when she was my teacher. Finally my mother and I convinced him it would look good on my college applications, and it would be better to go than to sit around the house all summer, bored out of my mind.

My mother sits on my bed. 'My little girl, going away for the entire summer. I don't know what I'm going to do.'

'Maybe you and Dad won't argue so much with me gone. Isn't he always saying you two'd never fight if it weren't for me?'

She sighs. 'Marcy, come on. Let up a little. He's had a rough time lately. He's been trying since we all went for counselling. You're the one who won't give him a chance. Why don't you try to forget the past and live in the present?'

'He wasn't trying last night when he screamed at me for coming in late. That's not the past, is it?'

She sighs again. If they ever hold an Olympics sighing marathon, my mother'd win, lungs down. 'He wouldn't yell if he didn't love you. It's just his way. He was very worried. Last night, after we went to bed, he told me he'll miss you.'

'Sure.' I refuse to listen to the same thing one more time. 'If he loved me, he could find better ways to show it. Why did he say the things he did about how I'd be good comic relief for the campers and how I think "taking a hike" means running out in the middle of an argument.'

'Marcy, you're being a bit unfair. He thinks of camps as places for sports, being outdoors. You know those activities aren't high on your list of favourite things.' She starts to repack my suitcase, neatening it up. 'He just likes to tease. That's the way he tries to show affection. You have no sense of perspective about him. There's nothing he can do that's right in your eyes. You expect perfection from people.'

4

'Well, so does he. How come when I bring home a test with a grade of ninety-seven, he asks what happened to the other three points instead of saying I did well?'

'You should try to understand him before it's too late and you feel sorry.'

The same old story. Now I'm supposed to feel guilty.

Ever since my father had a heart attack when school began this year, I get scared he's going to die. Sometimes I wish he were dead, I hate him so much. But there's also a part of me that really does love him. My mother should only know how many nights I stay up late worrying and trying to concentrate on keeping him alive.

My mother gets up. 'I'm going downstairs now. If you need anything, call.'

After she leaves, I continue to iron.

I hate ironing almost as much as I hate taking gym, and that's a lot. Last year I had to take two gym classes to fulfil requirements and make up the one I'd flunked. Ironing and gym should be outlawed. Once my mother began working, we all had to chip in and help out more in the house. The words 'permanent press' took on a whole new meaning in my life after that.

I wish I were already at camp. Maybe I can get enough experience there so I can become an editor on the school paper, instead of just a reporter. Then I can get into a good college, study literature, live my own life, and become a writer. I don't care if my father says most writers don't make enough money to support themselves. I want to be a writer anyway.

And I have a goal for camp, a major goal. This summer, I've decided, I'm going to try to be a grown-up, so I'll be able to take care of myself. There's not much that happens that's really earth shattering when you're my age. You've just got to go on living, trying to get through every day. If my life were a novel, it would be one without much plot, just character development. So what I really want to do is develop my character, to try to grow up so that when I'm an adult, I'll be ready for anything.

There's a knock on my door. 'Marcy, it's me. Stuart. I want to come in.'

He opens the door after I say it's all right. My little brother's eight years old, and he still looks like a baby. At least he's got over his abnormal fixation with Wolf, a teddy bear he used to fill with orange pips. Now he's got this thing about becoming a football player. He wears his football helmet all the time, even to bed. I hope that someone invents a shampoo that can penetrate plastic before his head begins to fungus.

Once he's in my room, he yells, 'Lewis has the ball, sports fans, and he's heading into his own territory . . .' Stuart dashes around the room. 'No one can touch him. His feet are golden.'

He jumps on to my bed. 'They try to close in.' He jumps off and crawls under the ironing board.

'Hi, Stuart.'

He throws his arms forward and touches my feet with the football. 'A touchdown, sports fans. Lewis does it again.'

I humour him and yell out a cheer that the kids at school do during pep rallies, being careful that the hot iron doesn't fall on his helmet or on my bare foot.

Stuart gets up, dusts himself off, bows, and says, 'Thank you. Thank you.'

I grin at him. 'So what's new?'

'Why can't I go to camp with you?' he asks

for the zillionth time. 'Just iron a name tag on me and pretend I'm a stuffed animal.'

'You know why. I've got to work there, lead my own life.'

He crouches into position and yells, 'Hike.'

'Not that kind of hiking, Stuart. It's a camp for the arts, not for sports.'

'But your name's not Art and you are a good sport.'

I tap on his helmet. 'You're very silly.'

'I know, but you like me this way.' He stands up. 'Marcy, it's not fair. You get to do everything first, just 'cause you're the oldest.'

'You're getting on my nerves,' I say.

'I'm supposed to get on your nerves. That's what little brothers are for.' He grins. 'Well, I tried. If I start bugging everyone now, by next summer they'll send me to a camp too.' He throws his football into the air, yells, 'It's another great interception for Lewis and he's off.' He races out of the door.

Quiet. Finally.

Sure I get to do things first, but I have to do all of the fighting to get what I want. Then once I'm all done, he gets things at an earlier age. Being the oldest isn't easy.

I finish packing, fold the ironing board, and take it out to the cupboard.

My father's coming down the hallway. 'Marcy, let me help you with that.'

'I can do it myself,' I say, thinking about how he shouldn't put any strain on his heart.

He frowns. 'You never give me a chance to do anything for you.'

There's no way to win.

I say nothing.

He says, 'Take good care of yourself at camp. Your mother and I won't be around to watch out for you.'

I nod, holding the ironing board between us, feeling like a lion tamer who's losing control.

'Just be careful,' he continues. 'Don't try any funny-looking cigarettes or do anything that would make your mother and me unhappy.'

I wish he could tell me he loves me, instead of making me feel as if I'm going to screw everything up. I don't even smoke anything. Why can't he trust me?

He leans around the ironing board, kisses me on the forehead, and walks quickly away.

I stare at him as he goes down the steps.

He calls up to me. 'Don't forget to set your alarm for six a.m. I want to get an early start.'

I don't have to be there until eleven or twelve. The drive from New Jersey to upstate New York should take three hours, at the most. He always makes everyone leave early, to miss the traffic. We always end up hanging around. It's so embarrassing.

I shove the ironing board into the cupboard. It tilts down, hitting me on the head. As I push it back and shut the door, I want to cry – not because I got hurt by the board but because I have a father who just doesn't understand me.

Back in my room, in my own bed for the last time until the end of summer, I feel very strange. This time tomorrow I'll be on my own. Trying to be grown up. Not knowing anyone but Ms Finney. Being a CIT without ever even having been a camper. Not having a boyfriend back home to tell the other counsellors about. Missing the summer parties back here and the friends I've made. All of a sudden I'm nervous, not sure I'm doing the right thing. I can't believe it. I'm getting homesick before I even leave, homesick for a place I've always said I couldn't wait to leave.

In order to fall asleep, I attempt counting sheep. But it's no use. Not only am I wide awake, but all of the sheep have name tags sewn into their wool and they all know how to act more adult than I do.

Two

'Rabbit number forty-eight,' Stuart yells.

Whenever he sees a van, he yells 'Rabbit'. It keeps him busy on long trips. Otherwise he spends the entire time asking to stop at bathrooms.

I stare out of the car window.

My father's shut all of the windows, turned on the air conditioner, and lit one of his smelly cigars.

I cough a little.

My mother says, 'Martin. Please. That cigar smells like burning chicken feathers – and you know you shouldn't smoke with your heart.'

'Stop babying me,' my father grumbles. 'Anyway, I don't smoke with my heart.'

'Rabbit number forty-nine,' Stuart yells.

I see the sign. THIS WAY TO SERENDIPITY.

My parents are yelling at each other as we pull into the driveway.

I want to die. What if someone hears them?

The time. It's nine forty, and there doesn't seem to be anyone around. Too early. For once I'm glad, because no one will hear my parents fight.

They continue to yell at each other.

'I hate those cheap cigars.'

'These aren't cheap.'

'Well, they smell like fertiliser.'

'Okay, stop it,' I yell. 'Please, we're almost there. Don't ruin this for me.'

My father stops the car in front of a huge stone and wood building, three storeys tall. It looks like a castle owned by a middle-income king. There's grass and dirt and trees all around with huge empty fields, soon to be filled with people. It's definitely not suburbia.

There's no one in sight, and the place looks as if it goes on for ever and ever. There's not a streetlight. I bet there's not a shopping mall for miles.

I don't even see any cabins.

Everyone in the car's still pouting.

Finally my mother says softly, 'Martin, I just want you to take better care of yourself. I don't want you to become a statistic.'

My father nods. 'Smoking is one of the few pleasures in my life, though.'

I feel sad for him, all of a sudden. Then I notice it's quiet. Peace. Another truce.

We get out of the car and look around. To the right of the car park there's a tennis court, a basketball court, and an area for volleyball. Oh no. Just like gym.

'Marcy,' Stuart yells. 'Goats. Real goats.'

I look. There really are five goats, standing by a large bell.

'Those are probably the kids assigned to your bunk.' My father grins.

Stuart jumps up and down. 'Kids – kids are goats – I get it. Very funny.'

'Your father likes *kid*ding around,' my mother joins in.

Sometimes my family gets very corny, me included.

'Sounds like you're both butting in.'

Stuart lunges at me, headfirst. 'Butt, butt.'

I stick my hand forward, to protect myself, and his football helmet bends back my finger.

I yell.

Both of my parents rush over.

My finger's starting to swell.

'Marcy. I'm sorry. I didn't mean to hurt you,' Stuart says.

'It's okay,' I say.

'Marcy, is that you?'

It's Ms Finney, coming out of the building with some guy.

I run up to her.

We hug.

She's grinning. 'You look wonderful. You've lost so much weight. But then I always thought you looked good.'

My family joins us.

Ms Finney says, 'Welcome, everyone. I'd like to introduce you all to my husband, Carl.'

My father reaches out to shake hands, saying, 'Mr Finney. I'm Martin Lewis.'

'Pleased to meet you. My last name's Klein; Barbara and I've kept our own last names.'

'It figures,' my father says, sort of under his breath, scowling and backing off.

'I'm sorry I'm so early,' I say.

'I'm not,' Ms Finney says. 'It'll give us some time to talk before everyone else arrives.' She grins.

Mr Klein says, 'Let me get your bags. We can load them into the van now and take them up to your bunk later.'

'A van. Where? It'll be Rabbit number fifty,' Stuart yells.

Stuart, my father, and Mr Klein go over to the car to get my stuff.

My mother says, 'How are you doing, Ms Finney? I've often thought of you.'

She answers, 'I'm doing well, very happy. My master's degree is completed. Carl and I've been married for six months now, and we love working at this camp. We were here last year and have the chance to do lots of new things. It's like a dream come true, to be at a creative place.'

'I'm so glad you're at a place where you're not hassled,' I say, thinking of the trouble she had at school.

She grins at me and then turns to my mother. 'How are you doing?'

My mother says, 'It was a little rough for a while, with my husband's heart attack, my job, and taking courses at the local college. But I'm managing. We're all managing.'

I think about how well she's done, even stopped taking tranquillisers.

Mr Klein, my father, and Stuart return, followed by the goats. 'The bags are in place,' Mr Klein says. 'Barbara, we'd better finish up our work before everyone arrives.'

'Carl and I'll be working in the main office, Marcy,' Ms Finney says. 'Join us after you say goodbye to your family.'

Everyone says goodbye to them and off they go, arm in arm.

I hope that someday I can be just like Ms Finney, perfect and happy with someone.

We all look at each other.

My mother starts to cry.

Stuart yells, 'I don't want to leave. Let me stay here. You can mail my clothes.'

'I'll write to you every week,' I say.

'You don't have to write to me. I'm staying.' Stuart holds on to my legs.

My mother says, 'Write every day.'

I nod. I'd promise to write every hour just to get all of this over with.

They unloosen Stuart from my kneecaps.

We all stand there.

Finally my mother says, 'I guess we should go,' and sniffles.

My father says, 'Let us know if you need more money.'

I feel so mixed up – glad that they're finally going and afraid to be left alone.

Stuart runs towards the basketball court, screaming, 'You're going to have to capture me to get me to leave.'

With my father racing after him, my mother starts to shout, 'Martin. Be careful. Your heart . . .'

Stuart stops short and returns with his head hanging down.

I feel sorry for him.

My father comes up, puffing a little.

'Are you all right?' I'm scared.

He waves away my question. 'You worry too much.'

Stuart yells, 'Touchdown,' and runs up as if he's going to tackle me but hugs me instead.

I pat him on his football helmet.

It's time to say goodbye.

My mother hugs me.

My father pats me on my head and says, 'I think we'll stop off in Woodstock and do a little sightseeing.'

They get into the car and leave, screaming goodbyes.

I feel deserted. Now that I'm alone, I'm not so sure I can cope. What if it turns out to be an utter disaster?

I look around the camp. It's beautiful. Any place this great looking can't turn into a disaster. But I bet people said that about the *Titanic* too.

I head for the main building and go inside. It must be the dining hall with all the benches and tables set up. There's even a fireplace.

The goats follow me.

Do goats eat people?

One of them starts to bleat.

Now I've done it.

Ms Finney bounds down a set of steps on the other side of the room.

A goat rushes over to her.

'Get out. You know you're not supposed to be here.'

'I'm sorry,' I say. 'I thought you said to come in.'

'The goats, not you, Marcy.' She laughs. 'Come on. Let's get these beasts out of the dining room before the Board of Health decides to make a surprise visit.'

The goats get turned around and pushed out of the building. I've never touched a goat before. Ms Finney obviously has. She's better at it than I am.

Once the goats are gone, I say, 'Ms Finney, I've really missed you. Since you left, there's no teacher I've had who's anything like you. It's so good seeing you, even if I'm expected to touch mangy goats.'

'The goats give milk for the children allergic to regular milk. Listen, since I'm not your teacher any more, please call me Barbara. Everyone else does.'

'Okay . . . Barbara.'

She rushes on. 'I'm so excited about this summer. We'll put on plays, dances, concerts, publish writing, show artwork. It's going to be wonderful.'

I smile, thinking of how lucky I am to be here.

She twirls around. 'I just can't wait. But now, we've got to finish getting ready. We're stapling papers for the first meeting. Would you mind helping out?'

'Not at all.' I feel a little formal, no longer at home, not really a part of this place, even though she's being so friendly and bubbly.

I follow her up the steps and think of what a secret coward I am, how afraid I am of everything.

How the goats will eat me.

How scary it is to meet new people.

It's not easy being so frightened of everything. And when I think of how much I've improved in the last year, I wonder when I'll ever get finished with making changes and be really grown up.

Before I have a chance to think of any more terrors, we're at the top of the steps and Ms Finney – Barbara – heads into an office, where Carl's running papers off on the duplicator.

'Marcy. Carl.' She claps her hands. 'Now you'll have a chance to get to know each other.'

Another fear. Men. I'm always afraid they're

going to yell at me like my father does. Or be as unreasonable as Mr Stone, my high school principal.

Carl smiles. 'Barbara's told me so much about you.'

I say, 'Nice meeting you,' and stare at the floor.

Barbara says, 'The others'll be arriving shortly.'

'How many?' I ask.

'Thirty-three staff members and one hundred and twenty campers.' I knew the campers wouldn't be arriving for another week. 'That gives us a chance to do staff training and to set up the camp.' Barbara picks up a stack of papers and hands them to me.

I staple them and think about the new staff members, hoping we'll all get along, that everyone doesn't pair up but me. I wish again for a boyfriend back home, so I wouldn't feel so alone. There was Joel for a while, but his father decided they should move to New Mexico. It wasn't a great romance, but it was a good friendship. I miss him.

My mood must show, because Barbara, who has been putting papers in piles, comes over to me. 'Are you all right?'

I try to smile. 'Does everyone at this place know each other? The staff, I mean.'

She smiles back. 'Some are returning, some are new. Carl teaches ecology at a local college and gets staff members from there. Some are from other places. Don't worry. I've got a feeling everything's going to be perfect. We've planned so long, so carefully, so hard, made some changes. Nothing will go really wrong.'

Carl says, 'Barbara's the eternal optimist, always positive things will be wonderful. Marcy, by the end of the training week everyone will know everyone else. Everything will go well, I hope.' He crosses his fingers.

Feeling calmer, I smile a real smile.

We all go back to our jobs.

I staple.

Carl sorts.

Barbara piles.

I look at them. They look good together, happy. Barbara's hair's grown down to her waist. He's got a beard.

I staple my finger.

The points are in my index finger. How gross.

It hurts.

Carl looks up to see why our efficient system is no longer working.

I look at my finger. It's the same one Stuart bumped into.

Barbara comes over.

I still haven't said a word, waiting for the gangrene to set in. It doesn't really hurt much, but I figure that's because it's paralysed or something terrible.

'Oh, Marcy,' Barbara says. 'Does it hurt much? Let me get some tweezers from the infirmary.' She rushes out.

I look at Carl. 'You must think I'm awfully dumb.'

He shakes his head. 'I once slammed my hand in a car door. Things happen.'

Barbara returns, pulls out the staple, wipes off the spots of blood with rubbing alcohol, and puts a Band-Aid on it.

'Marcy, I think you're going to live.' She grins. 'I bet I could have even pulled it out with my fingers.'

'No amputation? I'm so glad. I was afraid my writing career was over.'

Carl says, 'The first casualty of the camp season. I only hope the rest are so minor.'

I pull up the Band-Aid and say, 'Minor? It looks like a baby vampire has got me.'

Barbara laughs. 'Or one of the bats that live in the top of this building.'

Bats? I never even thought of bats. Now I've got a new fear to add to my long list.

Cars are honking below, suddenly.

'Hip, hip, hurray,' Barbara yells, jumping up and down. 'Camp's begun.'

I follow Carl and Barbara downstairs and wonder whether anyone's ever been sent home for an acute case of stapled finger.

Three

Everyone's arrived. I've met my head counsellor and seen my bunk. I wonder if it's too late to change my mind and go home. This is a little scary and strange.

I'm stuck with the upper bunk bed. Corrine, as senior counsellor, gets first choice.

Some night I'll probably roll over, fall out, break several bones, and have severe internal injuries and bleeding. Or a rung of the rickety ladder will crack when I'm climbing up, and I'll fall on my head and get a concussion.

Corrine immediately puts a picture of herself and a guy on her cubby.

I put a writing notebook on mine.

As we unpack, I sneak looks at Corrine. She's

got curly blonde hair, bright green eyes, and an incredibly thin body, fashion-model skinny. I bet she can eat anything she wants without gaining an ounce.

She says, 'Barbara tells me that you're a wonderful writer. I'm so glad. This year I want us to help the kids gain confidence in writing. I also want us to help them put out great newsletters and magazines, as well as their individual work.'

'Me too,' I say.

She continues. 'I'm a journalism major at college. Someday I want to be an investigative reporter.'

Funny. I thought sure she'd want to work on a fashion magazine. I've got to remember not to stereotype, not to look at someone and make instant judgments. I hate it when someone does that to me, yet it's something I do, especially when someone's skinny.

A bell rings below.

'We can finish unpacking later,' Corrine says, grabbing a notebook. 'Staff training's about to begin.'

I grab my notebook. 'Do we get detention if

we're late for the first meeting? Do we have to stay after camp and wash the volleyball court?'

Corrine laughs. 'You'll have to follow the goats around, pick up after them, and be in charge of their once-a-year bath.'

'Let's get a move on,' I say.

We rush out the door and down the steps. Lots of other people are also coming down the hill from their cabins.

Halfway there, someone yells, 'Hey, Corrine.' Corrine stops. I stop with her. She waves to this absolutely gorgeous blond male who is by the pool, pulling something out with the skimmer.

She yells, 'Hello, Jimmy. What did you catch?'

He pulls the skimmer out of the water and comes over to us. 'It's a skunk. Want to give it mouth-to-mouth resuscitation?'

Corrine makes a face.

Jimmy turns to me. 'Want to give me mouth-to-mouth resuscitation?'

I stare at his mouth.

Corrine says, 'This is Marcy Lewis, my CIT. This is Jimmy, camp Romeo.'

'Hi,' I say.

I want to say: If there are going to be auditions for the person to play camp Juliet, put my name on the list. But I don't have enough nerve. With Jimmy's looks I bet everyone in the world wants to go out with him.

The bell rings again, this time a lot, like someone means business.

'We'd better hurry,' Corrine says.

'I'll see you later.' Jimmy looks at me.

I try not to stare back at him although I'd love to.

As Corrine and I head down the hill, she says, 'I wasn't kidding about Jimmy. He's a bit of a flirt.'

I think that I kind of like being flirted with, especially by someone as great looking as Jimmy. He almost makes me want to get over my fear of men.

Everyone's gathered around the bell, the goats included.

It's obvious a lot of people know each other.

There's a lot of hugging and kissing.

I stand off to the side and notice I'm not the only person who doesn't know people.

Someone rushes up, hugs me, and says, 'It's so good to see you.'

I stare at her, not sure who she is.

'Don't panic. My name's Heidi Gittenstein. I just got bored standing around and not being a part of this.'

'I'm Marcy Lewis.'

She says, adjusting her baseball cap, 'Let's go around and do this to everyone else who's still standing around.'

It's a crazy idea. I love it.

I run up, hug someone who's still standing alone, explain what's happening, and then we both go off to hug someone else.

Soon everyone's running around, hugging everyone else.

I have a feeling I'm going to like this place.

Barbara yells, 'Everyone inside.' We go into the dining room and sit down at tables.

Carl quiets everyone down and announces, 'Since this is the first meal of the summer, Barbara and I've decided to give you a special treat – pizza and soda for lunch. Purchased out of our own meagre salaries.'

There's wild applause and foot-stomping.

Pizza. I love pizza. Pizza with extra cheese, pizza with mushrooms, with sausage. Pizza with pizza. I've got to be careful, though, not to eat too much of it or within minutes I could probably gain back every lost pound.

I take one piece.

Soda gets passed around. I take a Diet Coke.

I could mug for another pizza slice, but don't.

Once everyone's done and only empty white boxes sit on the tables as evidence, Carl and Barbara stand up and hand out the stapled papers.

'You can read this later,' Carl says. 'We want to start right in on our training session.'

I feel an arm on my shoulder. Looking to the side, I see it's Corrine. She's smiling at me. I smile back.

Corrine seems so nice, I think as I listen to Carl. I wonder why she acted kind of weird about Jimmy.

'I want each of you to pick a person whom you don't know and spend five minutes talking to that person.'

It's like I'm back in Ms Finney's, Barbara's, class. She used to do stuff like this.

Jimmy comes over to me and says, 'Want to be partners?'

I debate saying, Yes, forever and ever, but instead say, 'Sure.'

I feel like Queen of the Prom.

We go off into a corner, to the left of the fireplace.

'I hope we get to know each other better,' Jimmy says, giving me this sort of sexy smile.

I can't believe it. Here I am, Marcy Lewis, former girl blimp, sitting with this absolutely gorgeous guy who acts as if he really does want to get to know me better.

All my life I've dreamed of something like this.

Nancy, my best friend back home, told me I've really changed a lot in the past year, that I look good, but it's kind of hard to believe after you've spent your whole life resigned to being Ms Grotesque Lump. But nobody here knows that, except for Barbara.

Jimmy continues. 'Don't listen to anything

bad that Corrine might say. I think she's got the wrong opinion of me. I'm really a wonderful human being.'

'Do you carry around letters of recommendation?' I ask.

He grins. 'In my cabin. You'll have to come up and see them sometime.'

'I suppose you also do etchings,' I say.

'Actually I play the piano.'

'And the field too,' is the comment of someone who has come over to join us. 'Hi, my name is Mel. We're supposed to enlarge our groups.'

Mel joins us. So does Heidi, the girl who came over and hugged me. We all talk for a while.

'Two more groups unite,' Barbara yells.

Now there are eight of us, all finding out about each other.

'Everyone back together now.'

We get back together, only this time we all seem to crowd in closer.

I kind of wish I were sitting next to Jimmy, but he's sitting next to Heidi, looking into her eyes.

Carl points to Heidi. 'Who knows something about this person?'

Corrine yells, 'She's from Washington, DC, a senator's daughter.'

'She's an artist,' I add.

'She wants to be president someday.'

'So how come she's at a creative arts camp?' someone wants to know.

Heidi answers, 'I want something secure to fall back on if I don't make enough money as a painter. Presidents pull in good salaries.'

More people yell out stuff.

I look over at Jimmy.

He winks at me.

Carl points to someone else and everyone makes comments.

He points to me and people say things, all nice. About my writing, my personality, and my sense of humour. What a relief.

No one knows what I was like before. I can be what I want to be, not what people expect or think they know. I always worry that people expect me to be something I'm not when I'm not even sure of what I am.

Finally all staff members are discussed. It's

really great. Even though I don't know all of the names, I've got an idea about each person and it's going to be easier to get to know everyone.

'Break time,' Barbara yells. 'Bug juice.'

Everybody stamps their feet and applauds again. I do too even though I'm not sure why.

Gallons of something that looks like Kool-Aid are brought out.

I take a glass. It's sort of like water with a little Kool-Aid sprinkled in.

In her letter to me Barbara mentioned that the camp was not a rich one, but she never mentioned that we'd have to live on coloured water.

I hope my mother can send up a care package of Coke.

I notice that Jimmy's talking to another one of the new female counsellors.

After the break we role play.

The experienced counsellors pretend to be campers with an assortment of problems.

The CITs have to show how to solve the problems.

I get a counsellor named Lori who pretends to be a mosquito-bitten camper and is screaming how she wants to go home.

I pretend to put Calamine lotion on the bites.

'What else?' Barbara asks.

I pantomime putting the cap back on the bottle.

'Scratch them for the kid?' someone yells.

Corrine says, 'Hug the kid.'

I do.

Barbara nods. 'That's it. Just remember that the kids are going to want some attention and will do lots to get it. They'll need a lot of affection. I know that we all do, but remember, the kids come first. I want each of them going back home feeling special.'

Role playing continues for a while.

Then Carl and Barbara explain the basic rules. How many days off. Procedures. Responsibilities. How no one is supposed to use drugs or get drunk. What to do in case of emergencies.

Barbara looks at her watch. 'Time for general clean-up. Get the cabins ready for the kids. Then we'll have a cookout supper and campfire.'

Everyone troops out.

Jimmy and Carl are talking to each other

about how to handle the skunk smell in the pool.

As Corrine and I walk back up to the cabin, I ask Corrine what comes next.

'This camp has got to be cleaned up after the winter. We did it before we left last year, but there's always sweeping and stuff.'

Housework, actually bunkwork.

We go back to the cabin. I sweep the floor, and Corrine gets the spiders' webs down.

I look down at a corner of the room. There are all of these tiny brown pellets.

'Corrine, what's this?' I call her over.

'Mouse turds,' she says.

'Bullshit,' I say, figuring it's some kind of curse they say at her college.

She comes over and punches me on the arm. 'Very funny, Marcy.'

I look at her, then realise she's not kidding around.

They really are mouse turds.

I think I'm going to throw up.

But at least it's mice and not bulls.

I wonder if bats make pellets too.

I feel like Dorothy in *The Wizard of Oz*, when

she turns to her dog and realises that she's far from home.

Well, Toto, I guess we're not in New Jersey any more.

Four

Camp's wonderful. I only hope it stays that way once the campers get here later today.

I lie in bed, listening for the patter of little mice feet. So far so good. No more pellets. No sounds.

It's quiet outside. Birds singing.

Corrine snores.

The clock says six a.m. I think it runs in my family's genes to be early risers. I decide to go out before work starts.

Work. We've been cleaning the entire camp, getting supplies ready, holding more workshops, playing lots of games. For a camp stressing creative arts, there's certainly a lot of physical activity. Carl says it 'enriches the whole person'.

My body hurts from all the enrichment. My blisters have blisters.

I quietly climb down the ladder, dress, grab my soap, towel, and blow drier. Corrine's warned me to be silent until she's had her first cup of coffee.

The door creaks when I open it. I catch it before it slams.

No one else seems to be up.

I've got the bathroom to myself. Usually all the females in camp seem to be using it at the same time. It's as bad as taking a shower after gym.

Finishing up, I go back to the cabin, sneak inside, and put my stuff away.

Corrine's still snoring.

I didn't think skinny people snored.

I grab my notebook and pen and go outside again. It's beginning to get really light.

Two-thirds of the way down the hill, between the cabin area and the main building, there's a good tree to sit under to write the daily letter to my family. The pool's towards the left, the fields are on the right. The main building's down below. I owe four letters. Things are too busy. I can just imagine what it's like at home. My mother will rush every day, anxiously checking the mail. When no letter arrives from me, tears'll come to her eyes. At first she'll imagine the worst. She'll think I've been captured by a band of demon bats or fallen off a mountain. Then she'll get upset and angry. I've really got to make this a good letter to make up for not sending the others.

I write a lot, big, so that it takes up lots of room. It's hard. I'm not sure what I should say. I want to have some privacy, also there's not much to really report. Does she want to hear about my blisters, about my crush on Jimmy, about Corrine's snoring? What do you say about camp to someone who's not there to get the whole experience?

I do my best, filling up four pages and putting them by my side.

There's a goat standing right next to me. It starts to eat my letter. Then it takes off down the hill with all of the pages in its mouth.

Someone behind me laughs. 'I've heard of people having to eat their own words, but that's ridiculous.'

I turn around and see Ted Chaback, one of the CITs. He's carrying his guitar.

'I bet that really gets your goat.' He grins.

Oh no, more goat jokes.

Ted sits down next to me. 'Relax. We'll rewrite it. What was it? I'll help.'

'It's just a letter to my family. I promised to write every day and haven't. That animal just ate a week's worth of news.'

Ted says, 'Why don't you start out with: "Dear Family, I've just met a wonderful human being and while we're not planning to elope, I think I'm going to like going out with him. His name's Ted. You'll love him."'

I look at Ted. He's cute, brownish-blond hair, blue-green eyes. He's been in some of my training groups and we've kidded around but never really talked. I know that he's a senior in high school and from Connecticut.

'I think we'd better stick to telling them about the cookouts and stuff,' I say. 'I'd hate to announce anything prematurely.'

'Give it time.' He grins again.

We write the letter together, each contributing every other line. It doesn't make much sense, but it's fun to do. Being with Ted is fun. Usually I'm kind of shy around boys, but he's easy to get along with.

People are beginning to go down the hill.

The breakfast bell rings.

Ted and I race down. He beats me, by a lot.

I collapse on the grass. 'I'm really not in shape for this.'

'I like the shape you're in.' Ted smiles.

I blush. I'm not used to this.

Jimmy comes up to us. 'Ready for the invasion of the campers?'

I nod, still out of breath.

The campers are really arriving today, after lunch.

Jimmy moves on to talk to Ryan Alys, one of the guys on the grounds crew.

I stare at Jimmy.

'One of the smitten, I see,' Ted says.

I look at Ted.

'It happened last year too. At least half the females fall in love with him.'

I blush again.

'You'll develop better taste soon and see that the only person Jimmy loves is himself.'

Ted raises his eyebrows.

The bell rings again for breakfast, and we go inside.

Corrine and Mark, Ted's head counsellor, are sitting together and we join them.

'Ready? The kids'll be here soon,' Corrine reminds me.

'Can't we just keep camp the way it is?' I beg.

She laughs and shakes her head. 'The moment of truth, the final camper lists, will be here shortly.'

Barbara comes over to our table, says, 'Morning. Bunk assignments. Enjoy your day,' and hands us the cabin rosters.

Mark says, 'No problems evident on my list. Can't wait till the kids get here.'

He looks over Corrine's shoulder at our list. 'You've got Ginger Simon? What's she doing in with the eleven- and twelve-year-olds? Why are you stuck with her?'

'Sandy said she wouldn't take her again, even if it meant losing her job. You know how Barbara can convince you to try anything. So I said we'd take her, but should be given danger money.'

I sit there listening. How come no one asked

me about taking a problem camper? I guess because I don't know the kid. 'What's the problem?'

Corrine shrugs. 'I'm not sure. I know her parents are divorced and that she's got a real chip on her shoulder. But she's a fine artist. Last summer she did some really nasty things, was cruel to a lot of people, and was a general disturbance. Barbara wants to give her another chance though, thinks maybe we can reach Ginger and help her.'

'Barbara's always involved in causes,' Mark says. 'I don't think this is going to be one of her better choices.'

Ted says, 'Let me know if I can help.'

I have this funny feeling in the pit of my stomach. How can they doubt that Barbara's right? Am I wrong to think everything she does is perfect? Maybe I can show them all and be the one person who is able to reach and help Ginger.

I scrape off the burnt parts from my French toast and cover it with syrup. Calories that will go straight to my hips.

Corrine finishes and says, 'I'm going out for a

quiet walk. It's probably going to be my last chance of the day. Marcy, I'll meet you back at the bunk to finish getting ready.' She waves goodbye.

'Smile, Marcy. Ginger is only one twelfth of the cabin. It'll be all right.' Ted pats me on the arm. 'And I'll be around to give you a hand.'

Mark laughs. 'After you finish working with our seven- and eight-year-olds. That's not going to leave you with much spare time. Although something tells me that you're turning into a charter member of the Marcy Lewis fan club.'

It's Ted's turn to turn pink.

Mark looks at me. 'You must have some special power, Marcy. This young man was much admired by many last summer but spent the entire time with the kids and working on his music. I've never seen him act like this.'

'Man cannot live by guitar alone,' Ted says and grins at me.

My turn to blush again. 'I guess that makes me your pick,' I say. 'Guitar pick, get it?'

Everyone groans appreciatively. I guess I'm handling this okay, but I wish I'd brought my brother's teddy bear, Wolf, with me. I could use it now. I bet Wolf would love to be filled with bug juice.

Five

Countdown. They'll be here any second.

Barbara and Katherine, the nurse, have set up a registration table on the lawn in front of the main building.

Corrine's up at the cabin. I'm waiting to greet our kids and then bring them up to her.

The first car arrives and stops. The parents emerge and try to pull a kid out of the backseat.

He's screaming, 'Don't leave me here. I promise to be good. I won't even ask for my allowance. I promise. I'll practise my clarinet at home every day.'

I think of Stuart, who'd give anything to be here.

Barbara walks up and starts talking to the kid.

Ted comes up beside me and says, 'I bet he's going to be in my bunk. He looks the right age – about eight.'

Sure enough Barbara calls out, 'Ted, come here and meet Max.'

Ted walks over, puts his arm on Max's shoulder, and they go up the hill.

More cars drive up, more parents, more kids.

It's an epidemic.

Counsellors are running up and down the hill, bringing kids and gear to the cabin.

'Marcy, here's someone for you.'

Barbara says, 'Marcy Lewis, Linda Allen.'

I grin and the kid grins back.

Her parents stand there saying things like, 'Please, remind her to write to us,' and 'Make sure she eats her green vegetables.'

I nod.

We take her trunks over to the area designated for our bunk so the truck can bring the baggage up later.

As Linda and I walk up the hill, she says, 'What's red and green and goes one hundred miles an hour?'

I shake my head.

'A frog in a blender.'

Gross. But funny, in a sort of sick way.

'I'm going to be a stand-up comic,' Linda offers. 'I've come here to try out my material and to learn how to perform in front of groups that aren't my family.'

'I hope that you never do that joke in front of a group of ASPCA members.'

'What's red, green, and *brown*, and goes one hundred miles an hour?'

I sigh. 'I don't know and I'm not sure I want to know.'

Linda grins. 'The same frog a week later.'

It's a good thing my stomach's had a chance to settle from breakfast.

We get to the cabin. I take Linda inside to meet Corrine and then start down the hill again.

Linda yells, 'What's green and makes loans?'

'Chase Manhattan Pickle,' I yell back.

As I continue down the hill, I wonder whether all of her jokes are going to centre around the colour green and whether her whole family is fixated on that colour. Money, vegetables, frogs, pickles. I bet she's got some jokes about the Incredible Hulk.

By the time I get back to the registration table, there are four campers waiting, saying goodbye to their parents and talking to Barbara.

Three of them are 'old-timers': Ellen Singleton, Betsy Zolt, Alicia Sanchez. They tell me I don't have to lead them up the hill, that they know the way and can lead Robin Wiggins, a new camper.

I watch the three go up the hill, arm in arm, with Robin sort of hanging back.

Maybe I should have gone up with them anyway. It's not always easy to know what's the right thing to do.

Ted walks up. 'Surviving?'

'Yup. Except for having to listen to some frog jokes. How you doing?'

'Fine. One of the kids is a bed wetter, though, and he brought up a rubber sheet. Some of the guys were making fun of him.'

'What did you do?'

'Took the kids who were doing the teasing aside and talked to them. And put the kid with the problem in a bottom bunk. I was told a joke too. What's got a red nose, white face, and lives in a test tube?'

'What?'

'Bozo the Clone.' He grins.

I groan.

'Marcy,' Barbara calls out.

I run over.

'Marcy Lewis. Risa Hess. Helene Gerver.'

I welcome them.

Risa's mother says, 'Please make sure that she wears her retainer at night.'

Her father says, 'And that she doesn't lose it. I'm sick and tired of replacing them.'

From Helene's mother I hear: 'Make sure that Helene gets to bed on time. And don't forget she needs a little night-light.'

'Oh, Mom,' Helene looks down at the ground. 'Stop embarrassing me.'

I take out my notebook and write down the instructions.

'Can't we come up and inspect the cabins?' Mr Gerver asks.

'Sure,' I say.

'I'll be all right. Come on. Let me go up without you. Nobody else's parents are going up,' Helene begs them.

'We just want to make sure everything's all right.'

Helene looks up in the air. 'They'll probably want to look at my honeymoon suite when I get married.'

Mr Gerver laughs. 'Okay, we won't come up. Kids. They always think we baby them too much.' He looks at the other parents.

Helene nods.

I take Helene and Risa up the hill.

We pass Jimmy, who's putting chemicals into the pool.

Risa runs up to him, grabs him by the legs, and yells, 'This year I want to be one of your girl friends.'

He grins and pats her on the head. 'In a few years.'

Helene and I just stand there watching.

Risa starts jumping up and down. 'I'm so glad you came back. I was afraid you wouldn't be here, that there'd be no one good to have a crush on. And I'm old enough now. Look, I even got my braces taken off.'

She smiles at him.

He examines her teeth.

'She's still got to wear a retainer at night,' Helene says.

Risa glares at her.

I laugh. I can't help it.

Jimmy says, 'I'll put your name on the list, Risa.'

'Use indelible ink,' she says.

'What's your name? I'll add yours too.' He turns to Helene.

'Zelda Pinwheel.'

I've got a feeling I'm going to really like Helene.

As we continue up the hill, Risa yells, 'Don't forget, Jimmy. I'm going to be a famous actress someday. You'll be able to say that you "knew me when".'

We get up to the bunk.

The old-timers hug each other, and I make sure the new kids are introduced.

Corrine gets them to start making a sign for the cabin.

I leave, head down the hill, and wave back at Jimmy, who is standing in the sun, working on improving his tan.

I wonder if my name's on his list and what the number is.

There are four kids waiting when I get back to the table.

Barbara says, 'Marcy, except for Kitty, all of these young women are here for the first time. Be sure to point out all of the important landmarks to them.'

I get the names first. Janie Weinstein. Kitty Amoss. Bobbie Caputo. Stacey Reed, who is carefully carrying an instrument case.

We start up the hill.

'Don't forget the important landmarks,' Janie giggles. 'I'm from New York City and camp there means something totally different.'

I look at her and laugh. 'Okay, city slicker, I'll show you the wilds of New York State.'

I stop at a tree. 'This is a tree. You can tell by the bark, by the leaves on it, and because it grows out of the ground. It's not a counsellor because it doesn't have a whistle around its neck.'

'We've got trees in Central Park. Only there's usually a mugger behind them.'

We check, discover no mugger, and continue

with the tour. 'This is a goat.'

'I knew it wasn't a counsellor, no whistle.' Janie nods.

'It looks like my study-hall teacher from last year,' Bobbie offers.

'Who is that absolutely adorable boy?' asks Janie, pointing.

I look up expecting to see Jimmy, but it's Ted. He's holding a crying kid in his arms.

We go up to them. Ted is talking to the kid.

'Alvin, this is my friend, Marcy. Marcy, please tell Alvin that goats don't eat people.'

I start to laugh until I take a look at Alvin's face. He's absolutely terrified. Tears are streaming down his pale face.

'They don't bite. I promise. Sometimes they nip, but that's just play. It won't hurt.' I figure I've got to tell him the truth. 'Just don't leave paper around them.'

Stacey tugs on Alvin's sneaker. 'Watch me.'

She slowly moves to the goat and pets him.

I'm so glad the goat stands there calmly.

She turns around. 'See, it's all right. Honest. Let me carry you and show that he won't hurt.

Marcy, please hold my flute. Carefully.'

I nod and take it.

Alvin clings to Ted for a minute and then goes into Stacey's arms.

He looks so tiny . . . and very scared.

Stacey stands by the goat, not moving.

Alvin's holding on for dear life.

Finally she stoops down and starts to pet the goat.

Alvin keeps his head buried in her shoulder. Finally he turns around and looks at the goat.

Janie whispers to me, 'Will they be all right?'

I nod as Ted puts his hand on my shoulder.

Alvin nervously looks and then puts his head back on Stacey's shoulder.

Finally he looks again and slowly puts his hand out to touch the goat.

The goat nuzzles him with his nose.

I relax. I only wish my letter had been so lucky.

Alvin gets out of Stacey's arms and moves closer to the goat.

After a few minutes Stacey takes Alvin by the hand and brings him back to Ted.

Ted says, 'You handled that well. Do you know many goats?'

'No, but I've got a younger brother,' Stacey says.

Alvin hugs her leg. 'Be my friend.'

She nods and pats him on the head.

'You were great,' I say, handing her back the flute. 'Now I think we should head up to the cabin and get settled.'

Ted says, 'I'll see you later,' takes his hand off my shoulder, and grins at me.

As we go up the hill, Bobbie says, 'Is that your boyfriend? You sure are lucky.'

'Ted and I are just friends.'

Why do eleven- and twelve-year-olds ask so many questions?

We arrive just as the truck comes up with all of the suitcases, sleeping bags, and trunks.

A girl from the maintenance staff, Annie, is driving. 'All of your kids are here except one and we're not sure she's coming. So we decided to bring this up so the rest of you can unpack.'

'Who's the last one?' Betsy asks.

'Ginger Simon,' Annie says.

'Oh, no,' yells Ellen and pretends to throw up.

Every other returnee has the same reaction.

'How come we're stuck with her? She's supposed to be with the younger kids, isn't she?' Betsy wants to know.

Corrine says, 'We've got her. That's enough of that reaction now. People can change. Maybe she has. I want you to give her a chance . . . and I also think you can set a good example since you're older.'

'Now you sound like my mother,' Risa says.

Corrine continues. 'Well, I mean it. We want everyone here to have a good time. We also hope everyone learns how to get along with people.'

'Ginger's not people. She's an animal,' Risa says.

'Try,' Corrine says.

'Okay, okay,' the old-timers grumble.

'Let's get unpacked,' I suggest.

Everyone brings the stuff inside and puts it away.

The kids look at what each other brought and talk about swapping.

Corrine and I go into our little room.

'I knew it wouldn't be easy when they found out about Ginger.' Corrine makes a face.

'Maybe she's changed,' I say.

'You're just like Barbara, always looking on the bright side.' Corrine smiles. 'Well, maybe she has. Maybe we'll get lucky and she'll decide not to come back.'

We go out to the kids.

Janie's taking an upper bunk with no one underneath it. 'This will be my penthouse apartment. In case the dreaded Ginger doesn't return, I can always turn it into a maisonette, two floors, with the lower bunk for parties.'

Corrine returns to our room and comes out again, carrying a bag of lollipops. 'Who wants one?'

Almost everyone yells, 'Me.'

Bobbie says, 'Thanks, but I don't eat things with sugar. It's bad for you.'

'Me neither.' Ellen shakes her head. 'And I don't eat meat either.'

'Since when?' Risa asks.

'I became a vegetarian last year.'

'Ugh,' says Linda.

Everyone but Bobbie and Ellen grabs a lollipop, yelling, 'I want cherry swirl.' 'No orange.' 'No raspberry.'

'I can't make up my mind.'

'One each,' I yell. 'Save your appetites for dinner.'

Kitty says, 'Unless things have changed drastically, I'd rather not. Has the food got any better?'

Alicia giggles. 'Oh, Kitty. You always complained about the food and then ate four servings.'

Four servings. How can she be so thin?

The door swings open.

'Well, here I am. Bet you were all hoping I wouldn't show up.' In walks a frowning kid. Her fringe is practically covering her eyes, and her hair is plaited in pigtails.

'Welcome, Ginger. Have a lollipop.' Corrine holds one out to her.

'A bribe? No thanks. I brought my own stuff. If you don't take anyone else's things, you don't have to share your own. Where's my bunk?'

I point to the one beneath Janie.

'I don't want a lower bunk. I was here last year. I should get to choose before one of the new kids.'

'Whoever gets here first, gets to pick. You know that,' Corrine says.

Everyone's standing around, not saying a word. Standing real straight. Kind of nervous and angry.

Janie's sitting on the top of her bunk.

Taking the lollipop wrapper off, she says, 'Oh well, there goes the maisonette.'

Ginger turns to Stacey. 'Guess you must be one of the scholarship kids. They always let some of you in.'

I'm shocked.

Stacey takes a step backwards.

Ginger continues, 'I should get your bunk. My father pays full price. I'm not a charity case.'

'You're disgusting,' Betsy says.

'Thank you,' Ginger says. 'I just love compliments.'

Stacey quietly steps forward.

It's all happening so fast. I don't know what to do.

'Just because I'm black doesn't mean my parents can't afford to pay.' Stacey looks like she's going to cry.

I think about how wonderful she was with Alvin. I wonder how Ginger can say something like that.

Kitty tosses her blonde hair and says, 'As a matter of fact I'm here on a scholarship, and I'm not giving up my bunk for a little creep like you. You were trouble last year and I can see you haven't changed.'

Ellen goes up to Stacey and puts her arm around her shoulder. 'Don't judge the rest of the campers by this rat.'

Alicia says, 'Last year she told me I should go back to Puerto Rico and leave America to the Americans. When I tried to explain that we were part of the US, she called me a rotten name. Ignore her. She's not worth it. They should never have let her come back.'

Corrine says, 'Ginger, I want to talk to you privately.' Grabbing her by the arm, she takes her outside before anyone else can react.

The room's absolutely quiet. Everyone seems frozen into place.

I try to think of what Barbara would do. 'I think we should sit down and talk about our feelings about what just happened.'

Everyone looks at each other.

Finally they sit down.

'I think we should just totally ignore Ginger,

pretend she's not here,' Kitty says.

A couple of the kids agree.

'Maybe she's got a lot of problems that make her act that way,' I say.

'We all have problems. That's no excuse,' Janie says.

'Marcy, you don't know how terrible she can be.' Ellen frowns. 'Last year they almost sent her home, but they decided to give her another chance, the suckers.'

Stacey says, 'I don't want you to ignore her because of me.'

'If I were you, I'd want them to pour honey all over her and put her on an anthill,' Betsy says.

Stacey bites her lip.

Betsy leans over to Stacey and says, 'Do you want to swap lollipops for a while? I'm getting tired of this flavour.'

Stacey smiles and makes the exchange.

Soon everyone with lollipops is either swapping or licking each other's lollipops.

My mother would die if she saw this.

I trade with Robin.

My mother would make me wash my mouth

out with twenty bottles of Listerine. She won't even let everyone use the same bathroom cup.

The bell rings for lunch.

Everyone seems to be in a better mood, in some ways closer because of what happened.

We all rush out of the door.

I can see Corrine sitting under a tree, talking to Ginger.

I've got a feeling that it's going to be some summer, that I've got a lot to learn . . . and I'm going to have to learn it quickly.

Six

Lights out. It's definitely time for that. The campers may not be exhausted, but I am absolutely wiped out.

It's been a long day, a very long day. The preparation, arrivals, getting them settled, taking them to the pool to be tested, to the showers after swimming, back to the bunk to change and go over the cabin rules, on to dinner (noisier than the school cafeteria ever was), a meeting so that the campers could meet the staff and learn the general rules and regulations.

The campfire. I hope marshmallows come out of hair or else Ginger's going to attract a lot of flies. Somehow, someone managed to drop a freshly melted marshmallow on her head without getting caught. No one would admit to having seen who did it, not even Ginger. She wouldn't let Corrine or me try to help her get it out.

I tried to talk to her, but she turned away.

Now we're back at the bunk.

There's lots of giggling going on. It began as soon as we turned out the lights.

Corrine walks into our room. 'I've suggested they all settle down and go to sleep, but I doubt they will. After all, it's the first night, to be expected.'

'What should we do now?' I ask.

'Why don't you work on the diary we're supposed to be keeping. Just relax a little.'

I get the notebook and look at the first-camp-day assignment. We're supposed to write down first impressions of each camper, a little description of each of them, and my own feelings and perceptions about the first day.

I begin by opening the notebook and staring at it. That's what happens when I confront a blank sheet of paper when I begin writing. I go as blank as the page.

I alphabetise the names then doodle on the margins.

Risa sticks her head in the door. 'We're taking a poll to see who in the cabin has already got her period and how old they were when they got it. Do you two want to be part of it?'

Corrine chuckles. 'No, and I think you should cut it out. It's time for lights out, and anyway that may embarrass some of the kids.'

Risa shakes her head. 'The poll's already taken, six yesses, with the youngest age being nine. Four noes. One maybe. And one, 'if you don't leave me alone, I'm going to beat you up'.'

'Let me guess,' I say. 'The last one's Ginger.'

'It sure wasn't Stacey,' Risa says.

'I think that's enough for tonight, Risa,' Corrine says. 'Lights out.'

'We took the poll in the dark. The only light on in this cabin's yours.'

Linda sticks her head in the door. 'I think this camp's haunted.'

'Why?' Risa asks.

'Because everyone here keeps talking about the camp spirit.'

'Out,' Corrine and I yell. 'Get into bed.'

Risa and Linda vanish, giggling.

Corrine gets out of her bunk and stands up. 'Marcy, please watch any comments about Ginger. If the kids think we can't stand her either, they'll just come down harder on her.'

I nod. 'Okay. I'll try. I'm sorry.'

'Don't be sorry. It's understandable. Just don't do it again, if you can help it.'

'Okay.'

Corrine pretends to pound her head on the wall. 'I need a break. First days wipe me out,' she says. 'Marcy, you're in charge. See you in ten minutes . . . or so.'

She leaves. I'm going to have to try harder to be nice to Ginger. Setting an example is hard when you're only a couple of years older than the campers. Being the youngest CIT isn't easy. Still I'm glad that Barbara thought enough of me to ask when they needed a last-minute replacement.

I stare at my notebook for a few minutes and then write.

The day's been really hectic.

Corrine returns. 'Your turn to go out.'

I yawn. 'I'll skip it tonight. I'm exhausted.'

She grins, 'I ran into someone outside who wants to talk to you.'

'Who?' I ask, jumping out of my bunk without even using the ladder.

'It's Ted. I'm glad you got over your crush on Jimmy,' she says while I put on my sneakers. 'I didn't want to butt in before, but I know what he's like. I went out with him once last summer. It's just not worth it. You spend the entire time listening to him talk about himself.'

She crawls into bed. 'I feel much better now that I told you. I feel like you're the little sister I never had, but always wanted.'

'I'm glad you've adopted me. I always wanted an older sister.'

She grins. 'Now go outside and say hello to Ted. And Marcy, don't do anything that I wouldn't do.'

I wave and walk outside.

The kids are still giggling and talking to each other in their beds.

Ted's standing near the cabin, looking at the sky. It's glorious in the country. Clear. Stars. There's even a full moon tonight.

I come up behind him, tap him on the

shoulder, and say, 'Pardon me, sir. Is this space taken?'

He turns around, smiles, and says, 'Hi, Marcy.'

After that wonderful start I've got no idea what to say next.

'I just wanted to see you, find out how your first day went. I hope I haven't disturbed you.' He looks a little uncomfortable.

I hear giggles from the direction of the cabin. We move to a more secluded area, where we won't be the cabin's late-night show.

We sit under a tree.

I slap at my arms, killing the mosquitoes who think I'm the local blood bank.

'So how did your first day go?' I say.

'Fine. And yours?'

'Okay.'

'This is a wonderful conversation,' Ted says. 'For two people who were hired for their creativity, this is really dull.'

I giggle. Giggling must be catching. 'I'm sorry. I guess I'm just feeling a little overwhelmed . . . by camp.'

'Not by me?' Ted grins. 'Well, good then. I

FIRST DAY IMPRESSIONS- Marcy Lewis

NAME	# of years	Impressions
1. Linda Allen	0	cute short brown hair. BAD JOKES! Wants to be a comic-actress.
2. Kitty Amoss	3	Medium height, blonde, stood up to Ginger- no sugar. Writes.
3. Bobbie Caputo	0	Tall, curly brown hair, kind of quiet, no sugar. artist.
4. Helene Gerver	0	Long straight brown hair, great looking, green eyes, seems quiet but has sense of humour- actress
5. Risa Hess	5	curly short brown hair, talks alot, flirts, a leader. actress & writer.
6. Ginger Simon	2	brown hair, fringe, pigtails, awful. THE PITS!!! artist.
7. Stacey Reed	0	corn silk hair, cute, nice to little kids. MUSICIAN
8. Alicia Sandez	3	brown hair, bi-lingual, assertive, nice, DANCER
9. Ellen Singleton	3	Tall, very thin, vegetarian ARTIST (pottery)
10. Janie Weinstein	0	curly brown hair, braces on teeth, funny, bright. Maybe person who dropped marshmallow on ginger. Wants to be writer, dancer, MUSICIAN, artist.
11. Robin Wiggins	0	very quiet. Don't have clear picture of her in my mind.
12. Betsy Zolt.	5	Good at getting kids together, watches a lot. DANCER.

A B C D
E F G H I
J K L M N O
P Q R S T
U V
W X
Y
Z

CAMP IS FUN, TIRING, AND

CONFUSING!

MAP OF CAMP

TREES

LONG DRIVEWAY.

MAIN BUILDING

CARL LEARDAN'S HOUSE

SPORTS AREA

BELL

GOATS

Field

TO CABINS

POOL

HILL   HILL

CRAFTS WRITING PRACTICE BUILDINGS

TO CABINS   TO CABINS

GIRLS BATH-ROOM & SHOWERS

TO CABINS

BOYS BATH-ROOM & SHOWERS

73

can handle that as long as I know that the diagnosis is overwhelmed due to occupational hazard.'

As we sit there, I see Jimmy walk by with one of the girls who is on the grounds crew. He's got his arm around her waist and he's pointing something out in the sky.

I'm glad that's not me. Tonight at the campfire Jimmy asked if I wanted to go back to his room later to look at the newspaper clippings he's got about his sports triumphs. He asked while we were trying to deal with the marshmallow in Ginger's hair, I said no. Rlsa volunteered to go in my place, but Jimmy just looked at me, said, 'Your loss,' and left.

Ted pinches me on the arm and says, 'Marcy.'

I look at him.

'I don't think you've heard one thing I've said for the last four minutes.'

'Oh, Ted, I'm sorry.'

He shakes his head. 'You were too busy looking at Jimmy. I can't believe you could be turned on to that creep. I thought you had better taste.' He stands up. 'We'd better get back to our cabins.'

I jump up. 'It's not the way you think it is. Don't be mad at me.'

He says, 'I'm not . . . Well, maybe I am. I don't really know exactly what I'm feeling. I just think you're special and it makes me angry to think you like Jimmy better than me.'

'But I don't,' I say and realise that it's absolutely true. 'I do care about you, not him. I'm just a little confused.'

'Marcy, I want us to be friends. At least friends. Probably more.'

At least friends. Probably more. This thing with Ted isn't a crush. It's something more for me too, only I'm not sure. What if I let myself start to care and get hurt? I'm not sure I can survive a broken heart. I get hurt so easily anyway, so I've never let myself get too close to a guy, not that there have been that many opportunities. I'm scared. What if it turns into a real relationship and it's as bad as my parents' marriage?

I look at Ted. He's bright and fun and very cute. He's one of the nicest people I've ever met. He likes me, obviously a lot, and he's not afraid to let me know.

I push the hair out of his eyes and say, 'Friends. At least friends.'

He puts his arms around my waist.

I bet he's going to think I have no waist at all, that I'm just a puffball. Then I remember, I'm not fat any more.

I put my arms around him.

A mosquito's draining all of my blood out of my right arm, but I decide now is not the time to slap it.

We kiss.

It's wonderful.

We kiss again

It's still wonderful – until the large flashlight beams on us, we hear a cough, and separate.

It's Carl and Barbara, who are smiling.

I could die of embarrassment.

Ted says, 'We're on a ten-minute break. The cabins are supervised.'

Carl says, 'We're just doing our nightly check of the areas, to make sure everything's okay.'

'Everything's okay,' I say.

'So I noticed.' Barbara smiles.

I blush.

'About time to get back, isn't it?' Carl says.

Even though our parents aren't around, I've got the feeling that Barbara and Carl keep an eye on things.

I'm not so sure that's bad.

As Carl and Barbara go off to check out the camp area, Ted puts his arm around my shoulder and we walk back to the cabin.

I feel good. A little nervous but good.

We stand by the cabin for a minute.

I hear muffled giggling.

So does Ted because he leans over and gives me a fast kiss and whispers, 'I'll see you tomorrow.'

As I walk into the cabin, there's applause and a lot of voices start singing:

MARCY AND TED, SITTING IN A TREE

K-I-S-S-I-N-G;

FIRST COMES LOVE

THEN COMES MARRIAGE

THEN COMES MARCY WITH A BABY CARRIAGE.

Corrine's standing there, singing with the kids.

I look at everyone, wave as if I'm a queen

greeting her subjects, and walk into my room as everyone applauds again.

Seven

Two weeks of camp gone already.

Linda and Risa organised a midnight raid on the kitchen.

Kitty's been taking extra food from the dining hall and hiding it under her bed, in case hunger strikes late at night. We found a mouse under her bed. Stacey brought it to the nature shack.

Crying a lot from homesickness, Bobbie said she's allergic to bug juice and wanted to leave. Now that she's having fun, her allergy has disappeared and she's consuming large quantities of bug juice.

Alicia's teaching everyone to swear in Spanish.

Ellen's circulating a petition, protesting about

the amount of meat served. She wants a choice for vegetarians.

Ginger's been brutal. I tried to talk to her one day and she told me to 'bug off'. Another time I put my hand on her arm and she pushed it away. Only once was she ever friendly, the time that I suggested that she do some drawings for the camp magazine. When I asked her about the artwork later, though, she said, 'Who wants to work on that lousy magazine, anyway?' So I gave up.

I hardly have any chance to be alone with Ted. Camp's been in session for two weeks and while it's mostly fun, Corrine and I've been run ragged.

We've just called a bunk meeting.

Barbara's on her way up the hill right now to be part of the meeting.

The kids are sitting around, not saying much, playing jacks, writing letters, practising dance steps.

I look over my notes about what we're going to cover at this meeting.

Barbara arrives. 'Hi, gang. Let's get started.' She smiles.

Everyone looks at her.

'Why don't we hold the meeting under a tree outside?' Corrine suggests.

'Good idea,' Barbara says.

Outside we go.

Barbara takes out a clipboard. 'I understand some of you want the chance to air your feelings. Well, let's do it.'

The girls look at each other.

'I don't think it's fair that we have to go swimming,' Janie says. 'I don't want to learn. It's impossible.'

'But it's good exercise,' Barbara answers.

'Not when Jimmy's had to rescue me twice,' Janie says.

'Lucky.' That's from Risa.

Ellen raises her hand. 'I think the food here is nutritionally bad, too starchy, too much meat. Meat makes people act like animals.'

'I like meat,' Kitty says. 'Just because you don't, doesn't mean the rest of us have to live on rabbit food.'

'I'll give you my spinach,' offers Linda.

'Sugar's bad for us. There's too much sweet stuff given out.' Ellen won't quit.

'How come there's a rule that we can only get two candy bars a day from the canteen?' Janie makes a face.

'How about some rice and beans?' Alicia asks.

Barbara says, 'I want all of you to notice the differences of opinion here and see how hard it is to meet all of the individual needs.'

'You end up meeting no one's needs,' Robin says, pulling bark off a twig.

Sighing, Barbara says, 'We try.'

Stacey says, 'Someone put bubble gum in my flute. No one's been caught.'

'And someone cut the strings on my guitar.'

'My sculpture got destroyed.' Ellen is angry.

Corrine says, 'It's hard to prove who's responsible.'

Everyone stares at Ginger.

'I get blamed for everything. I don't have to take this.' Ginger sticks out her tongue. 'And I have a complaint too. How come you won't let me bring up my portable television? I'd rather watch that than have to be part of all the stupid group activities around here.'

'No TVs allowed. You know that.' Barbara stares at her.

'Rules are made to be broken,' Ginger smirks.

'No they're not.' Barbara shakes her head. 'Not the rules here. They're for your own good.'

'You've broken some rules in your life,' Ginger says. 'So don't play Ms Perfect with us.'

'Ginger,' I yell. 'Stop that.'

'It's all right,' Barbara says. 'It might as well be out in the open. I've been hearing a lot of that lately from a few people. It's better to get it all straightened out.'

She looks very tired but continues. 'I know I've taken some stands that don't go along with everyone's wishes. But I want you to realise, Ginger, that I felt that there were some very important issues at stake. It wasn't done lightly or without a lot of careful thought. That's different from the way that you've been acting, Ginger.'

'I don't see the difference.'

'Well, that's what we've all been trying to help you see.'

'Why don't you just leave?' Janie says. 'Good riddance to bad rubbish.'

'No name calling, please,' Corrine says.

Ginger says, 'Someday I'll be gone and then you'll all be sorry.'

'I doubt that,' Betsy says, speaking for the first time at the meeting.

Everyone looks at her.

She shrugs. 'Well, it's true. None of us would be sorry if Ginger left. I know she's the one who put peanut butter in my sleeping bag ... the crunchy kind.'

Barbara says, 'I really hope you can all learn to get along.'

'Dream on.' Kitty makes a face.

Linda says, 'We're making it sound like camp's terrible. I don't think it's that bad. I'm having a lot of fun.'

Of course she is, I think. She loves camp and kidding around. The other day someone told her that if you put a sleeping person's hand in warm water, that person would think she wet the bed. This morning I woke up with my hand in warm water.

'I like camp too. I just want a vegetarian diet,' Ellen says.

'I don't want to find bubble gum in my flute again, but I like it here,' Stacey says.

The kids continue to talk.

I keep waiting for Barbara to come up with

the magic solution, the thing that's going to make it all better.

It doesn't happen.

What does happen is that everybody gets a chance to talk out what's bothering them.

Barbara takes some notes and promises to consider the suggestions.

The meeting ends, and the girls go on to other activities.

I'm not sure what's been accomplished, except that I'm going to try again to reach Ginger, to do something no one else has been able to do.

Barbara puts down the clipboard. 'What a week. I'm exhausted.'

'It'll be okay,' I say.

She smiles. 'Carl would say you're beginning to sound like me, always sure that everything's okay.'

'That's what I tell her,' Corrine nods. 'Barbara, are you getting discouraged?'

Barbara nods. 'I figure that we've got a great place here – creative, open, sensitive to the individual – and still, people complain. Not only that, but we've had to send home two staff members for breaking the rules, smoking grass in their cabin. It's not been easy.'

'But think of all the good things happening here.' Corrine puts her hand on Barbara's shoulder.

'I'd like it to be perfect. How are we going to work all of this out? Where are we going to get the money to afford all these different foods? Vegetarian? Ethnic? No sugar? Some sugar?'

We sit quietly for a minute.

She speaks again. 'Is Ginger getting any better? Do you think she's responsible for all those problems?'

'Most of them.' Corrine nods.

'Maybe I made a mistake, letting her come back.' Barbara puts her head into her hands.

'You wouldn't do anything that's not right,' I say. 'Somebody may be able to reach her.'

'Marcy, stop making excuses for me. It's getting a little hard for me to be the perfect example that you want me to be. I'm really getting tired of it.'

'But . . .'

'Just get off my back,' Barbara says, standing up. 'I'm going for a walk.'

She leaves.

I feel stunned.

I really hurt.

The tears start.

I'm glad the kids aren't around.

Corrine says, 'Marcy, she didn't mean to hurt you. People sometimes say things without meaning them.'

'But she's really mad at me.'

'She's upset and just took it out on you. Marcy, you really do expect her to be perfect. You don't think that the people you care a lot about can make mistakes or be human. That's a heavy load to lay on someone.'

'I'm sorry,' I sniffle.

'You don't have to be perfect either. I know I'm not.'

'Sure, you are.' I smile at her.

'I snore. That's not perfect.' She's grinning at me.

'How do you know you snore?' I ask. 'You seem to sleep right through it.'

She grins more. 'I've had some comments and complaints.'

I grin back. 'Well, your snores are perfect, just the right decibels and very even. When I grow up, I want to snore just like you.'

'Surprise, my dear, you do snore.'

'Really? Nobody ever told me that before.'
I'm surprised.

'That's because you usually don't sleep with
anyone.'

I get up. 'I guess I'm just not as worldly as
you are. Have you had *many* complaints about
your snoring?'

'Nosy,' Corrine says, getting up. 'I'm not
going to answer that on the grounds that it might
incriminate me. Look, don't you have the
afternoon and evening off today?'

I nod, drying my tears.

'And a date with a very nice young man
named Ted?'

Again I nod.

'So go and get ready. And cheer up. It'll work
out. I'll come in to talk to you after I check on
the kids.'

I go back into the cabin and think about
what's been said. Maybe I do expect too
much of everyone. My mother tells me that a
lot.

I start to pick out what I'm going to wear.

There's a knock on the door.

'Come in.'

It's Barbara. 'Marcy, I'm really sorry.'

I stand there, holding a shirt.

'It's been a little rough lately. I'm sorry I blew my top.'

'It's all right.' I'm just relieved she's not mad at me.

'I want you to know the reason I got so angry is that I think sometimes we're a lot alike. I want too much perfection from myself and others too. There are lots of good ways we're alike and some not so wonderful ways. So I guess getting angry at you is a little like getting angry at myself.' Barbara plays with her hair, twirling some of it around her hand.

'I can think of worse things than to be like you,' I say. 'But I do understand what you're saying.'

'Good,' Barbara says. 'I'm glad we can talk about it.'

'Instead of yelling,' I say, thinking about how my father reacts.

'I'll see you later. Have a nice day off,' Barbara says. She smiles, waves, and leaves.

Being close to other people isn't always easy, but it's worth it.

Vacation. I need a vacation. All of this dealing with feelings. Working. Living with thirteen other people in the same small area. Being helpful. I'm wiped out. If I've got to finish off one more lanyard, I'm going to scream. Swimming. Hiking. Working on the camp paper. Cookouts. Getting ready for the talent show. Trying to keep the kids from killing Ginger when I'm not sure that I really want to stop them. Thinking of ways to try to reach her even though I'm afraid to try because she'll be mean. She's only ten, but she can be deadly. At night I'm so exhausted it's hard to fall asleep. The kids giggle. Corrine snores. I stay awake waiting for the sound of rushing mice feet and the swoosh of bat wings. I'd almost like to go off somewhere alone and sleep my time off away.

But I'm going to Woodstock with Ted. He's managed it so that we've got the time off together, and he's even arranged to borrow a car. A date with Ted, the use of the car. I wish everyone back home could see me now.

Corrine walks in while I'm getting ready.

'Marcy, why are *all* of your clothes on your bed? Are you planning on running away and can't decide on the proper wardrobe for your flight? Please don't desert me.'

I grin. 'I can't decide what to wear.'

'It's Woodstock. Denim,' Corrine says. 'Wear your jeans or something like that. You're not going to a prom.'

'I've spent the entire time up here in jeans,' I say. 'I want to wear something different. After all, it's my day off.'

'You just want to show Ted how pretty your legs are,' Corrine teases.

Janie runs in. 'Would one of you please remind the powers that be around here that I'm going to take the next bus back to New York City if they don't stop bugging me about learning to swim. If I were meant to be in water, I'd have been born with gills.'

Corrine says, 'Marcy, it's your time off. I'll handle this,' and she takes Janie outside.

I think about going to Woodstock. For years I've heard about it and I saw the film about the rock festival, which wasn't even held there. I've always wanted to go. It's supposed to be this

91

special place for the arts, for all different kinds of people. And now I'm going . . . and with Ted. I'm so excited that my stomach hurts.

I decide on my denim skirt, a light blue top, and stripey tights.

I grab my bag and walk out of the cabin.

'Skirt, eh?' Corrine raises an eyebrow.

Janie looks at me. 'You look nice. Big day off, huh? Bet you're going out with Ted. Be good. And if you can't be good, be careful . . .'

I can't believe she said that. When I was her age, I knew nothing. As a matter of fact I still don't know much.

Risu and Linda come running up to us. 'Did you see Nick? Did you? Did you?'

We shake our heads.

They're all out of breath.

We assigned them the job of camp gossip columnists, and they take their jobs very seriously. Only they spread the word before it's printed.

'Some of the kids bet Nick he didn't have enough nerve to shave his head. Now they've got to pay up.'

'You mean Nick, the counsellor, or Nick, the

kid in bunk nine?' Janie wants to know.

'The bunk nine Nick.'

The bunk nine Nick is coming up the hill, surrounded by a bunch of kids. Only now he's the bald bunk nine Nick.

'I only hope his parents aren't coming up on Visitors' Day,' Corrine sighs.

I look at my watch. 'I'll see you all later. I've got to go.'

I'm glad everyone's paying attention to Nick. Now I can make a fast getaway without any more comments.

Ted's waiting in the car park.

I get into the car.

He looks different, a little less like camp, a little more dressed up. Blue jeans, just washed and without the usual rips and tears. A short-sleeved T-shirt with the insignia from his sister's college, Princeton. Even his sneakers look like they've been washed.

Neither of us are wearing the usual layer of camp dirt that seems to collect on us as soon as we've been out for an hour.

'Did you see Nick?' I ask.

He nods. 'I'm afraid of what he'd have done

for twenty bucks.'

Ted starts up the car and heads out of the driveway.

We're on our way.

Eight

Woodstock, only eight miles from camp. Here we come.

'Do you have to sit all the way at the other side of the car?' Ted asks. 'I promise to keep both hands on the steering wheel.'

I move closer to him and look at the scenery.

He says, 'I think you're going to like Woodstock.'

'Corrine says there are some great places to shop. Do you like to shop?'

'Sometimes. When it's places I want to go and my mother's not along telling me what I should buy.'

I continue to look at the scenery.

'So what do you really want to be when you

grow up?' I ask and giggle. Giggling's truly catching. A regular plague. By the end of the summer I'll probably turn into a laughing hyena.

He says, 'A set of Tonka Toys. And what do you want to be when you grow up?'

'I want to be a kumquat.' I don't even know what a kumquat looks like. I just like the way it sounds.

'Are you sure?'

I nod. 'But if the job market's tough and there are lots of kumquats out looking for work, I guess I'll be a novelist.'

'I want to be a doctor, if I can't be a set of Tonka Toys. And no matter what, I always want to be able to play music.'

We grin at each other.

Getting into town, I see how small the shopping area is. I'm used to the shopping malls around my house. Ted parks behind the bank, and we walk to Tinker Street. There are lots of people around. Folks are sitting on the village green, talking, playing instruments, looking around, resting. Some of them look like pictures of the sixties, long hair, headbands. Some are wearing jeans, long skirts, dresses, shorts. It looks like anything goes when it comes to dress. Everyone looks summery. Comfortable. No one is wearing a prom dress. Corrine was right.

Ted holds my hand. 'Come on. Let's start at the library and work our way down.'

We walk along, swinging our hands and looking at everything.

The Woodstock Library is a wonderful little building, one storey, made of wood. It looks like a house that elves could live in.

'Let's go in,' I say. 'I love books.'

'Me too.'

We walk up the path. People are sitting all over the lawn, reading and talking.

We enter. It's great, really homey with librarians who smile and offer to help.

'I wish I could join even though I don't have much time to read,' I say.

'There's a bookshop farther up,' Ted says. 'We can stop there.'

As we leave, I hear one of the librarians talking to someone about the fair that's going to be run later on in the summer. Jumble sale, games, plays, good stuff like that.

We walk up farther.

There are lots of great shops, beautiful jewellery, clothes.

'Here we are,' Ted says. 'The Golden Notebook.'

In we go. I love the place. It's got natural wood, books all over, piled up on the floor, shelves practically up to the ceiling. By the nature section there's even a real spider weaving a web. I point it out to Ted.

'They probably pay it to be there,' he says.

'Maybe it's going through an identity crisis and thinks it's a worm – a bookworm,' is my comment.

I feel like a little kid in a toy shop. All those books. I've always wanted to be a writer, but before Ms Finney, Barbara, I was afraid to tell anyone. I think it's some kind of miracle that all we have to work with is the twenty-six letters of the alphabet. And they turn into words, sentences, paragraphs, chapters, books, conversations, plays. It's just incredible to me.

I buy three books. So does Ted.

We go through more shops.

'Here's one of my favourites,' Ted says,

stopping in front of a house. Rainbow Shop, it says.

We walk in. The place is filled with rainbows, stars, moons, unicorns. It's like being in a fairy tale.

The guy standing there smiles. He's wearing all this rainbow jewellery. He's even got an enamelled tooth with a star and rainbow on it. If I saw him walking down the street in my home town, I'd be a little surprised, but here it seems perfectly natural.

A woman walks up to us and hands us a piece of paper. 'Here's your rainbow.'

'Thanks.' I want to hug everyone in the world.

Ted starts to ask the Rainbow Man some questions, about the shop, about how he got started. I think it's wonderful that Ted's not afraid to talk to people.

The Rainbow Man's telling him about the time he said, 'I wish I had a quarter for every person who comes in here', and then decided to charge admission.

'I refused to work until he cut it out,' the woman who gave us the rainbow said. 'I went into the back room until he quit doing it.'

Everyone's smiling at everyone else.

I pick out a pair of rainbow earrings for me and a copy of *The Rainbow Book* for Stuart. I want to share this with him in some way. After all, he's stuck back home, and I just want him to be part of this somehow.

As I take the things up to the cash register, the Rainbow Man says, 'Would you like me to autograph the book?'

It dawns on me. He's the one who did the book. The real-live author. I'm in shock. A real-live author. And he seems like an ordinary person.

He signs the book.

As we leave the store, everyone waves goodbye.

Ted hugs me. 'Happy?'

'Very.' I hug him back.

He kisses me right there on the street in front of the world.

I'm too busy kissing him back to notice the world's reaction.

If my father could see me now, he'd probably lock me up in my room. But he's not here.

We stop kissing because I've dropped my

packages and have to pick them up.

Pizza next. The bulletin boards in the restaurant are full of news of upcoming concerts, plays, and art exhibits.

Next comes Rock City Rags, a place for T-shirts, where you can have anything printed on them.

'Let's get matching shirts,' Ted says. 'To always remind us of today.'

He's not afraid to say things like that. I come from a family that finds it hard to show feelings. It's so nice to be with someone who isn't.

We pick out the shirts. White. With the 'I Love New York' emblem put on it. Ted has his name put on the back with black lettering.

I say, 'I think I take a medium or a large, and I'd like "Marcy" put on with glitter letters.'

The saleswoman looks at me. 'Medium or large? I think you'll need a small. In fact, I'm sure of it.'

She and Ted are looking at me.

I can feel myself blush. Always blushing. It's disgusting. And it embarrasses me to have them look. Don't they know that blimps always take big sizes?

She puts a T-shirt up to me. 'I bet you've lost a lot of weight. People who do never have a really accurate picture of what they look like.'

The small shirt fits.

One of these days, when I grow up, I'm going to learn who I really am, what I really look like. But it sure isn't easy.

Even when I was heavier, I wasn't as bad looking as I thought I was. People usually aren't. But it's not an easy lesson to learn.

We leave the store.

Ted's got his arm around my shoulders, and I've got an arm round his waist.

All of a sudden I feel something weird around my hips, under my skirt.

It's my tights. They're starting to roll down.

I stop and pretend to look in a store window.

I put my hand into my skirt pocket and grab on to the tights to stop them from continuing the roll down my body.

We continue to walk.

One hand's holding on to my packages, the other's trying to hold up my tights. The hand that's trying to hold them up is attached to the elbow that keeps hitting Ted in his side.

Finally he stops and whispers in my ear, 'Want to tell me what's going on before I end up with a bruised and battered body?'

I whisper back, telling him.

He starts to laugh and can't stop.

I start to laugh too, dropping my packages, and try to hold up the tights with both of my hands in my pockets.

He just stands there looking at me.

'We have several choices,' I say. 'I can let them roll down and die of embarrassment. But then they'd have to find a new CIT and it's sort of late in the summer for that. Or we can find a place with a bathroom.'

Ted picks up my packages and says, 'There's a place farther up where we can get sodas. They have a bathroom.'

'Sounds good to me.'

We walk along. Actually Ted walks and I sort of hobble, legs close together, hands in pockets.

Finally we're there. It's a sidewalk café, and we sit down at a table.

Ted orders Cokes.

I creep into the bathroom, take off my sneakers and tights. Shoving the tights into my bag, putting my shoes back on, I imagine what it would have been like to have my tights roll down to my ankles in front of everyone. It's too awful to even think about.

I come back to the table.

Ted looks at my face and then down at my bare legs. He starts to laugh again.

So do I.

By the time we calm down, the Cokes have arrived.

We sip them and look at all of the people walking around. I love sitting in an outside café. I love Woodstock. I love the world. I love Ted.

I love Ted. Terror . . . happiness.

We finish the sodas and walk across the street.

Candlestock. The whole place is filled with all of these different kinds of candles. It's hard to make a choice.

I pick out a candle. Actually it's a beautiful bowl with a candle in it, one that can be refilled.

Ted's by the cash register, talking to the two guys there.

I continue to look around, at the sign on one of the shelves that says, SHOPLIFTERS WILL BE PROSECUTED BY THE LORD and at the candle that's taller than I am. Actually it's one that they keep adding to.

As I pay for my purchase, Ted introduces me to the two guys, Dennis and Martin.

Everyone's very friendly.

When we get outside, I hand the bowl with the candle in it to Ted. 'I want you to have this. It'll always glow, not melt down and be gone.'

He doesn't seem at all embarrassed by the gift. 'It's symbolic, like us, huh?'

'Writers are known to deal in symbolism,' I say.

We take the packages back to the car and then continue walking around town.

Then Ted and I drive all around. I sit in the car, daydreaming about what it would be like to spend the rest of my life here, the rest of our lives. I even have the names of our two future kids picked out. Heather and Dylan. Dylan because it's the name of one of my favourite poets, Dylan Thomas, and also the name of Bob Dylan, the singer who once was part of Woodstock. Heather because it just seems right for this place.

We stop by a stream, get out of the car, and go

down the banks and sit there.

For a long time we talk. It feels so comfortable. So right to be there with Ted. So this is what it's all about. Being in love. I don't want it to ever end.

We get back in the car, head back to town, and then sit for a while in the car holding hands and talking.

Dinner. Then a movie. It's fun, but I want to be alone with Ted, without other people around.

By the time we get out of the movie, it's very dark. There aren't any street lights.

'I guess we've got to go back,' I say.

Ted nods. 'Yeah, but I don't want to. Do you?'

I shake my head.

Another kiss. I think I've been kissed more times today than the total of all the times I've ever been kissed before.

This time, when I get into the car, I sit right next to Ted.

It's really dark on the road.

We drive along. My head's on Ted's shoulder. I put my hand on his knee.

He gives me a kiss on the top of my head and

says, 'Watch it. I've got to keep my mind on driving.'

I take my hand off his knee and move away.

'I didn't mean you had to leave. Are you always a person of extremes?'

I nod, move back, and just sit there.

We pull into the camp car park. Ted stops the engine, turns off the headlights, and puts his arms around me. 'Now I don't have to keep my mind on the driving.'

Reading books never really prepared me for how I feel. It's one thing to read about love and caring and wanting to hold someone and be held, but this is one time that the twenty-six letters don't come close to the real thing.

'Making out' is such a dumb expression for something so special.

Finally Ted says, 'This steering wheel's really uncomfortable. Why don't we find somewhere else to go? Like the back seat?'

I shake my head. 'I don't think that's a good idea.'

'Afraid?'

I nod.

He kisses me. 'Okay. Let's just sit here a few

minutes and relax.' He leans back.

I think about how wonderful he is. How I've always heard that lots of guys won't take no for an answer. But Ted's really nice. And I'm not ready yet. I know that. It's not just the question of what's right or wrong about sex. I know that right now it would be more than I could handle to actually 'go all the way' as the kids in the cabin always say.

I put my hand on his knee and say, 'I really care about you.'

He takes my hand off his knee and says, 'That's not going to help me to relax, to have you do that right now. I'm glad you care. I do too.'

More kissing.

'Want to reconsider your decision about not moving to the back seat?' he asks, touching my face.

'I keep reconsidering it, a lot. But no,' I say.

'Okay, then I think we should go back,' he says.

'Are you mad at me?'

'No. I just think it's best for us to stop now, if we're not going any further. Otherwise it's going to be very hard for me to maintain my reputation with you as "nice".' He pats my hand. 'Come on. Let's get going.'

As we walk up the hill, he says, 'Tomorrow morning I'll talk to Carl about giving us the same days off again for the next time, if you want that.'

I nod. 'I want that.'

We get to the cabin. Just as we start to say good night, we hear a lot of screaming coming from the bunk.

We rush inside.

There's a bat in bunk five.

Nine

There's a bat in bunk five!

It's flying all over the place.

I duck and feel like throwing up. What if it swoops down and its wings touch my face? Even worse, what if it bites me?

The kids are screaming, crying, and running.

Corrine's trying to kill it with a dust mop.

Ted grabs a broom.

One of my worst fears is coming true. There really is a bat. Just when things are going well, something happens to ruin it. It's like I'm being punished for being happy and doing what I want to do. That's why I'm so scared much of the time. Either things are going badly or they're going well and I expect disaster to strike.

The screams are getting louder. I think I'm one of the people screaming.

It's bedlam, absolute craziness.

Corrine trips over Robin, who's in the middle of the floor, curled up in a ball shape.

Stacey yells, 'Don't kill it. Let's try to catch it and make it the bunk mascot.'

Someone throws a Frisbee.

A Paddington bear flies through the air.

Ellen's trying to get it with her tennis racket.

Ted gets the bat.

Wham.

It falls to the floor.

He finishes off the job.

Crunch.

'I think I'm going to be sick. And they say New York City's rough. I'd rather have a cockroach than a bat any day,' Janie yells and heads outside.

Stacey starts to cry.

Ted comes over to me. 'That was some BATtle, huh?'

Carl and Barbara rush in.

'What's the problem?'

Corrine gets off the floor and points to the

mangled bat. 'Ted got it.'

'Good job, Ted,' Barbara says.

'I just happened to be in the neighbourhood and came to the rescue.' Ted bows.

'My hero!' I say. 'Perhaps I should be BATting my eyes at you.'

'I'll dispose of this,' Carl says, pointing to the bat.

'We've got to give it a funeral and bury it.' Stacey's still crying.

'I think its last wish was to be cremated,' Ted says.

'Bat killer,' Stacey says and steps on his foot. 'I'm never going to talk to you again.'

Barbara explains to her about how bats may carry rabies and that Ted did the right thing.

Ginger interrupts, 'And it might have been a vampire and sucked out someone's blood and driven that person insane. The person would then have brutally murdered every other person in this bunk and then committed suicide by throwing her body on a newly sharpened marshmallow stick.'

'Warped. You're absolutely warped. Look,

let's have the funeral and get some sleep. It's after midnight.'

Ginger continues anyway. 'The bat's brother and sister vampires are probably going to come here and try to avenge its death. They'll probably get all of us and we'll leave here with fangs.'

'I wonder if my orthodontist has ever made braces for fangs,' Risa says. 'Come on, Ginger. You're just being obnoxious, as usual. Isn't she?' She looks around, waiting for someone to say yes.

Barbara says, 'Ginger, I think you could put your active imagination to good use. Why don't you write some of this fiction down and submit it to the magazine.'

'She'd rather try to scare everyone,' Alicia says.

I think of how in the beginning I wanted to help her but haven't. She's so difficult. I don't think she knows when to stop, what's a joke and what's cruel. That makes me nervous.

Corrine brings out a shoe box and shovels the bat into it.

We all grab flashlights and go outside.

Everyone shines her flashlight on one spot, and Ted makes a hole in the ground with the broom handle. Then he puts the box into the ground and says, 'Now, somebody's got to say a few words.'

'Me,' Risa yells and begins. 'Dearly beloved, we are gathered here . . .'

'That's for weddings, dummy,' yells Ginger.

'No name calling,' Barbara says softly, putting a hand on Ginger's shoulder.

I expect Ginger to pull away, but she doesn't. In fact she places her hand on Barbara's.

Risa starts over. 'We are here this evening to mourn this dearly departed bat.'

'He's not dear,' Bobbie says.

'Well, he is departed. That's for sure.' Risa continues. 'While we did not know him for long, he will leave a memory in our minds.'

'Not in our hearts,' Helene says.

Janie pretends to cry. 'He looks just like he did when he was alive.'

'Except that he's squashed and dead,' Betsy says.

Risa continues, '. . . so we hope that he rests in peace.'

'Or pieces,' whispers Ted, coming up behind me and putting his arms around my waist.

The girls all start to go back into the bunk.

Bobbie says, 'I think we should bury the broom too. I'm never going to touch it. It's disgusting.'

'We'll wash it,' Carl says. 'Now, those of us who live in other bunks should think about going back to them. It's really late.'

'I guess he means me, since they've got a house and I'm the only other person not assigned to bunk five,' Ted says with a smile. 'Carl, don't you think I should get special visiting privileges since I saved the day?'

'Back to your bunk or I'll have you arrested for hunting out of season.' Carl points towards the boys' bunk area.

'And for carrying and using an unregistered broom,' I add.

Ted gives me a quick kiss good night and says, 'I'll see you tomorrow.'

Barbara turns to me. 'We're still friends, aren't we? You're not still upset about this morning, are you?'

I shake my head. 'No, I'm trying to learn that

we've all got the right to be human and less than perfect.'

'Except for me. Remember that I'm perfect,' Carl says.

Barbara shines her flashlight in his face. 'Okay, Mr Perfect. Then how come you left the coffeepot on tonight, forgot about it, and burned it out?'

'A momentary lapse.' He shines his flashlight into her face. 'Let's go home now.'

She nods and mumbles something about practice making perfect.

Corrine and I go into our room.

The girls have all quietened down and seem to be going to sleep.

As we change into our pyjamas, Corrine says, 'Boy, am I glad you two arrived when you did. Did you have a good time in Woodstock?'

'Wonderful.' I must have said or thought 'wonderful' a million times today.

We climb into our bunks.

I tell her about our day and how my tights rolled down. After we finish laughing about that, I ask, 'Corrine, how old were you when you fell in love for the first time?'

'Oh, it's that serious, huh? Well, the first time I was eleven and he was my fifth-grade teacher. The first time the love was mutual and serious was when I was fourteen. Boy, was that great . . . and very confusing, ending when his parents decided to move to Ohio. We swore our undying love but it's hard from a distance. After that, I fell madly in love with John, but he broke my heart. I still think about him sometimes, but it wouldn't have worked out in the long run. Now I'm in love with David. I really miss him. He's in France. We decided we needed some distance, some time apart. This love I hope is going to last forever. I even have the names picked out for the kids we'll have someday.'

I think of Heather and Dylan . . . Ted and my future kids.

I also think of the comment that Heidi once made about how she doesn't want any kids. But I do, I think. But not until I'm older, about twenty-seven, and have had a chance to do a lot of stuff.

Corrine says, 'I really think Ted's great. I'm glad you and he hit it off.' She turns out the light.

'Just remember that camp's going to be over and both of you live in different places.'

That's something I don't want to think about, not now, not tonight.

There's a lot more I want to ask Corrine, about being in love and sex, but I'm too shy to ask and I don't want to seem like a dumb kid, especially when she's treating me like an adult. It's hard to know who to talk to. I've never been able to talk much to my mother about it, even when she sat me down and told me the facts of life. Somehow that was hard because I kept thinking she and my father must have done it since Stuart and I are here, but it's weird to think of your parents having sex.

I'm not just shy, I'm tired, very tired. It's been a long day.

I'm almost asleep when I hear screams of 'raid' and someone playing a trumpet.

Suddenly the whole bunk is filled with kids from the boys' intermediate cabin.

The girls are screaming again.

I quickly jump out of bed.

Corrine grabs her dressing gown and puts it on.

I grab mine and do the same.

Opening the door, we get bombarded with water balloons and shaving cream.

Rolls of toilet paper are flying.

The trumpet's still playing.

Pillows are being thrown. Feathers are flying.

As quickly as it began, it's ended.

Bunk five's a disaster area. It's filled with toilet paper, water, and shaving cream.

There are also frogs running around, obviously collected and saved for just this occasion.

'Someone stole Paddington,' Stacey yells. 'He was my favourite stuffed animal.'

'I managed to bite one of them,' Ginger calls out.

Alicia curses in Spanish.

'Get those frogs out of here before I die,' Linda yells.

'Try catching them and putting them in a blender,' Helene yells back.

'Not funny.' Linda stands on her bunk. 'Please, if you catch them, I promise I'll never tell those two jokes again.'

The frogs are caught – I hope we got all of

them – and taken outside.

'Everything okay now?' Corrine checks.

'Someone stole my bra,' Robin says.

'Don't worry. You don't really need one anyway,' Ginger says. 'A Barbie doll's got bigger boobs than you do.'

'I'm going to kill her,' Robin yells, lunging at Ginger.

Corrine holds her back, while I say, 'Ginger, apologise.'

'Robin, I'm sorry you don't really need a bra.'

'That's not what I meant.'

Ginger sneers. 'Sorry.'

Some of the girls give Robin a hug and say things like 'Don't let her get to you,' and 'We should have made her eat those frogs.'

Corrine looks around the room. 'Let's get this all cleaned up and then we're going to have to go down to the showers to clean off.'

We clean up.

We troop down to the showers.

I'm past being exhausted. I'm not even sure I'm alive any more.

Everyone looks the way I feel.

Finally we all go back to bed.

It's finally quiet.

I wonder what Ted's doing right now.

The sheep I try to count are all jumping over rainbows. Frogs are hopping under those rainbows.

Someone from the bunk yells, 'Revenge will be ours.'

I hug my pillow, pretending the pillow's Ted, and fall asleep.

Reveille.

Someone should shoot the kid with the bugle. Or at least put a muzzle on him.

I'm tired. The only reason I can think of for getting up is to see Ted at breakfast.

That's enough of a reason.

I jump out of bed.

Giggling. I hear giggling. How can anyone be alert enough to coordinate their giggling mechanism after all of last night's disturbance?

I'm almost afraid of what I'm going to find when I open the door.

I peek out, into the righthand part of the cabin.

No one's there.

They're all on the left side.

'What's going on?' I ask, wiping the sleep out of my eyes.

All of the girls, except Ginger, are sitting together, looking guilty.

I repeat my question.

Risa says, 'We were just practising kissing.'

'Each other?' I ask.

'No, ourselves. Look.' She shows me her arm.

I look.

She's given herself a love-bite, a big red mark on her arm.

The rest of the girls hold out their arms. They've done the same to themselves. All of them have love-bites, red turning to purple.

'I didn't do it,' Ginger says. 'For once, I'm the good one.'

Corrine comes in.

'You two do it too,' Risa says. 'Then we'll all be alike, except for Ginger, and she doesn't count anyway.'

Ginger stomps off.

Corrine looks at their arms and then at me. 'Marcy, I have a feeling that today's going to be one of those days when I wish I'd taken another kind of job.'

I nod. But that's not really true. There's no place in the world that I'd rather be than Camp Serendipity.

'Okay. Get ready for breakfast,' Corrine says.

The girls try to convince us to give ourselves love-bites.

When we won't do it, they all sing, 'Every party has a pooper, that's why we invited you, party pooper.'

Finally we go to the dining room.

The girls are trying to give love-bites to all the boys in the bunk that raided us last night.

Corrine's right.

It's going to be one of those days.

Ten

Where's the time gone?

I feel like I've just got to camp and now it's half-way over.

The hiking. I don't think I've ever walked so much in my entire life. Back home, everyone walks to and from school and sometimes over to friends'. Other than that, our parents take us places in cars.

Not here. We walk everywhere. And as if that's not enough, Carl's some kind of nut about going on hikes. There have been three of them since the night that the bunk was invaded by the bat and by the boys from the intermediate cabin.

And the overnight. Some of the kids were

terrified. And those who didn't start out scared got that way after two hours of ghost stories.

Visitors' Day. Parents taking kids off the grounds, talking to us, making sure that the kids are having fun.

The swimming. Even Janie's learning to swim. And it's Ginger who taught her. Amazing. I still can't reach Ginger. I tried once more to be nice, but she told me to go away.

There's been kind of an uneasy truce for a while, ever since Corrine and I've been holding daily bunk meetings. I only hope it lasts.

And in another week it'll be time for carnival and the talent show . . . both on one day.

Ted and I are still 'going together'. That means the few minutes that we have free, we spend together. It's not really like back home where people get to go out on real dates. It's more like when people in grammar school and junior high went out (I always heard about it, but it never happened with me). People 'hang out' together, and everyone says they're a couple.

So now I'm part of a couple and I love it. It's not always easy, though, because sometimes I would like to spend more time with other people, and there just isn't enough time.

Especially with carnival and the talent show coming up.

It's been so busy here that there was barely enough time for me to even remember my birthday. That's why it was such a wonderful surprise, the party that Corrine and Barbara threw for me.

And the magazine. That's coming out this weekend too. With the hour and a half each day that the majors (dance, music, writing, art) have allotted, we've been getting the magazine ready, as well as the daily newsletters.

I'm watching the kids practise the bunk skit for talent night. They've put it together so that it's a showcase for their individual talents.

It's about a magic kingdom (only they've made it a queendom) where everyone is allowed to have one special talent and what happens when the people want to branch out and have more than one talent. The wicked witch casts a spell. They are, individually, unable to break that spell until they discover that as a group against the wicked witch, helping each other, they can make things end 'happily ever after'.

Risa says the skit's going to be a real show stopper.

Ginger says the only way it's going to be a show stopper is so that everyone can take time out to throw up. She's got the part of the wicked witch. I tried to talk to the kids about changing the script, but Ginger said she loved her part.

Oh well, you can't expect miracles.

I watch the kids practise as I work on the costumes.

Heidi Gittenstein stops by the cabin. 'Hey, Marcy, we've got permission to go into Woodstock after dinner to pick up some stuff for carnival. Want to come? It'll be you, me, and Sally.'

'I'd love to.'

'Great. We'll meet right after dinner.' She goes down the hill.

Great. It'll give me a chance to spend some time getting to know her and Sally better.

I continue to sew and try to remember if Ted and I've made any plans to be together after dinner. I doubt it, not formal ones. I don't think he'll mind though. It'll give him some time to practise his guitar, since he's always saying he doesn't have the time.

Ginger comes over. 'I've got some time free until I have to do anything again. Can I go brush my teeth? I've got some corn from lunch caught in my teeth.'

'Sure,' I say.

She rushes into the bunk for her stuff and runs to the bathroom.

Either she really is getting better or I'm getting used to her.

She comes running back, yelling, 'I'm going to kill someone.'

I rush over. 'What's wrong?'

She's angry. 'Someone put a pinhole in my toothpaste tube. When I went to use it, the gunk slopped all over me.'

'Calm down,' I say.

'I don't want to calm down. I've had it. Last night when I got into bed, someone made me an apple pie bed, and now this.'

'Why didn't you mention that at a meeting?'

'I didn't want to tell tales, but too much is happening.'

'Look, Ginger,' I say, 'I'll talk to Corrine about it after dinner and we'll try to work it out.'

She looks at me. 'Promise.'

'Sure,' I say, thinking that maybe now she'll be easier to reach. I would really like to be the one who helps her.

She joins the skit and I go back to sewing.

The other girls act like they're not responsible. I wonder who is.

Corrine's at the office, getting the literary magazine put together. I'll have to discuss it with her later.

The afternoon goes well.

Time to go back to the bunk so that everyone can write letters. Once a week every kid has to write a letter home and present the sealed message to the counsellor before dinner. That way we can see that mail is being sent home so that no parents complain.

The dinner bell rings.

Corrine comes up to me. 'I'm going to skip dinner tonight. I've got a fever or something. Do you mind?'

'I was supposed to pick up some stuff in town for carnival. Should I cancel?'

'I just want to rest for a while. I'll be fine after dinner.'

The kids are all kind of quiet at dinner, but I figure it's because they're all tired out from practising.

After dinner Ted comes over to me and says, 'Want to go for a walk after the tables are all cleared?'

I nod.

Heidi comes running over. 'Ready? Barbara says we can go now.'

I forgot.

I turn to Ted. 'Ooops, I've got to go shopping. Okay?'

'Does it matter if it's okay with me? Looks like you've already made your choice.' He shrugs.

I want to be with him. But I promised to go. And I do want to get to know Heidi and Sally better. It's confusing.

'See you around sometime,' he says in this really cold voice I've never heard before.

I start to say something but he's already turned away.

I watch as he goes over and starts talking to Betty, one of the other CITs.

That hurts – a lot. She's been after him ever since camp began.

Heidi looks at me. 'Wow. I didn't realise this was going to cause any trouble. Would you rather stay here?'

I'm not sure of what I want to do. Part of me wants to cry. Part of me wants to strangle Ted. How can I be so angry at someone I love so much?

Heidi turns her baseball cap to the back and says, 'Would you rather stay here, really? I'd understand.'

I look over at Ted. He's put his arm around Betty and they're laughing about something.

That does it. 'No, I want to go.'

We get into the van and Sally drives into town.

I try to put all thoughts of Ted and Betty out of my mind and concentrate on talking with Heidi and Sally.

After a while it becomes easier to join in their conversation.

I can even laugh a little.

Neither of them mentions what happened with me and Ted.

I'm glad because I might say something I would regret.

I remember that I'm supposed to talk to

Corrine about what happened with Ginger. Oh well, I can do that when I get back, or Ginger'll probably tell Corrine herself.

We pick up lots of stuff and then go over to a café, sit on the patio, and have Cokes.

'Do you play pinball?' Heidi asks.

I shake my head. In my home town the only kids who play are the kids who cause trouble.

'Want to learn? It's fun. We've got one at home,' Heidi says.

Pinball in the house of a US senator. I guess it's okay to play then.

We go into one of the rooms

Pinball machines.

There's a little kid playing.

Heidi, Sally, and I go over to one, Close Encounters of the Third Kind.

They're really good at it.

I'm not.

But it's fun. I love the flashing lights, the sounds it makes, and the way you don't think about anything personal when you're playing.

We play eliminations. I lose. They play for the championship.

I practise on another machine, feeding it quarters.

There's someone tugging on my Camp Serendipity sweatshirt. It's the little kid.

'Lady, want to play?'

Lady, he thinks I'm a lady. He's seven or eight so I guess he thinks I'm a grown-up. The little kids at camp are the same way.

A little kid. I bet I can beat him. He doesn't look tall enough to see over the machine. Maybe I've got a chance.

He continues. 'Loser pays for both games, after the first one.'

'Sure.' I'm sure I'll win, but even if I do, I won't make him pay for the next game.

We play.

Final score – 320,840 for him to 16,500 for me.

I've been hustled.

'Where'd you learn to play like that?' I ask.

'Tom's Pizzeria in New York City, near where I live and go to school. I play there a lot.' He grins. 'My name's Paulie. What's yours? Your turn to pay.'

I put in the quarters. 'I'm Marcy. How about teaching me?'

We play.

I pay.

He teaches.

I think Ted and I'll have to come here sometime and play.

Then it all comes back to me. Ted's mad at me, out somewhere with Betty. I bet he never talks to me again.

Heidi and Sally come over. 'We'd better get back. It's getting late.'

I wave goodbye to Paulie, who's getting more quarters from his parents.

He waves back.

By the time we get back to camp, it's dark.

We all go over to the staff recreation room. There are some people there, but no Ted and Betty.

Sally and Heidi go over to talk to somebody.

Jimmy comes over to me. 'Looking for Ted?'

I say nothing.

'I saw him go off with Betty. Why don't you and I go off for a walk?' He lifts one eyebrow.

'Thanks, but no thanks. I'd rather be alone,' I say and walk away from him.

I wave goodbye to Heidi and Sally.

Heidi comes over and whispers, 'Want some company?'

'I think I'm going for a walk. Thanks anyway.'

She nods. 'Just remember – the path of true love never runs smooth, or something trite like that.'

Once I get outside, I think about Jimmy's offer. Maybe I should have taken him up on it. That would teach Ted. But Ted probably wouldn't even care.

I feel as if someone has ripped my heart right out of my body.

I go off to the area where there are swings.

Corrine's on duty so I don't have to go right back to the bunk. I'm glad. I don't want anyone to see me right now, not when I feel like I'm going to split in two and want to die.

Sitting down on a swing, I start to cry.

It's all so confusing. I love Ted. He used to say he loved me.

Life can get pretty complicated, growing up. I used to think that if I were in love with someone who loved me, everything would be absolutely wonderful.

But it's not working out that way. It's so confusing.

I like being with Ted, having him hug and kiss me, hugging and kissing him. Sometimes I get nervous because I like the feelings so much and then I get scared that I'm not sure I'm making the right decision. But mostly I just like it.

Now, though, I feel as if I'm never going to stop crying, that all of the water in my body's going to exit through my eyeballs.

Someone sits on the swing next to me.

It's Barbara.

I try to stop sobbing but can't.

She says, 'Want to talk about it?'

I nod.

She waits for me to say something.

'I feel so dumb . . . and I'm trying so hard to be a grown-up. It's terrible.' I continue to sob.

'I know it's hard,' she says softly.

I tell her everything. How much I love Ted, how I set the goal for myself to be grown up, how hurt I am because Ted went off with Betty, how I'm trying so hard to do everything right with the kids that it makes me nervous, how confused I am.

'You shouldn't be so hard on yourself. It's difficult growing up. Carl and I always talk about what we want to do and be when we're grown up.' She smiles.

'You do? But you *are* grown-ups,' I say, wiping my eyes.

'Marcy, I'm not even sure what it means to be a grown-up. Everyone has moments when he or she doesn't feel adult. We're all concerned about doing the best thing and we've all had times when we're confused confronting new situations. You've really got to learn not to be so tough on yourself, to realise that lots of other people have the same problems. That doesn't mean that your problems aren't important, you've just got to learn to put them in perspective. You should try to progress at a comfortable rate without worrying about being perfect.'

'It just doesn't seem fair. I do the best I can. And still things don't work out. I feel as if I'm being punished all the time.'

'But you're not. It's life. Things happen.' She shakes her head. 'You know, Marcy – an example – I know there are times you hate your father.

But he really does care about you. When you hadn't written to them, he sent me a note asking if you were all right, just so they didn't have to worry. So you see he does care, even if you think it's unfair that he's not perfect.'

'How come you never told me?'

'He said not to. He figured you were busy, but your mother was "driving him nuts" with her nervous concern about you. And he didn't want you to think that he thought you were incompetent. You know, Marcy, he doesn't. He sounded very proud of you in the letter. So you see, you've got to learn to look at the whole situation. Did you do that with Ted, take his feelings into account?'

Thinking back, I realise I didn't, that I figured that he wouldn't mind – that I didn't have to check it out with him.

'Did you always have an easy time when you went out?' I ask.

She laughs. 'No. I made lots of mistakes. Maybe that's why Carl and I do so well together. We've both made mistakes and learned from them. Now we try hard to understand each other and listen.'

'I wish there was a magic pill that would make everything all better,' I say.

'But there isn't, and pills are not the answer. Working on things is.'

'It's scary.'

Barbara nods. 'It's the only way, and it gets less scary as time goes on. You've got to allow yourself the chance to work things out. You'll survive it. And there are some very good times to be had, just remember that.'

'Probably not with Ted. He hates me now.' I start to cry. 'Could you talk to him for me?'

'No.' She shakes her head. 'So many people make that mistake, trying to get a friend to be in the middle. You've got to confront him yourself.'

'I can't.'

She frowns. 'You're feeling too sorry for yourself. Of course you can. Look at how far you've come in the time I've known you.'

She's right. I used to be scared of everything when we first met. I can even deal with bats. Now I'm just scared of some things.

We sit and swing back and forth while I think about all that's been said.

All of a sudden I hear Carl yell, 'Come on,

Ted. Let's see how high they can go.'

I feel someone pushing me higher and higher.

Barbara's swinging higher and higher too.

'Are you okay?' It's Ted's voice that I hear.

'I want to get down. It's too high.' I slow down.

He helps me to stop the swing. I was a little afraid he was going to keep me swinging until I flew over the bars.

Barbara's stopped too.

She gets off and hugs Carl.

I get off and look at Ted.

We just stand there.

I want to yell, So, where's Betty? Where were you? But I don't scream. In fact, I don't say anything.

We stare at each other.

Carl says, 'Barbara and I'll be over at the volleyball court setting up. Be there in a few minutes. We're playing your team for the championship.'

Team. I'm not even sure we're talking to each other.

They go off, arm in arm.

Ted and I just look at each other.

I think about what Barbara said.

'Ted, let's try to work this out. I'm sorry I didn't explain that I was going into town. I guess I just didn't take your feelings into account. I should have talked to you about it.'

He looks at me. 'I'm sorry I walked away like that. I know you've got a right to do things with other people. It's just that all day long, the kids were driving me nuts and all I kept thinking about was that I'd feel better when I could be with you for a while. And then you were going off. I really wanted to be with you, to be with someone special, someone who didn't keep asking me to tie shoelaces or scream "There's a Fungus Among Us". Someone who didn't pretend to pull nits out of my hair. I just wanted to spend some time with you.'

'You didn't even give me a chance to explain, to talk it out with you. You went over to Betty.'

He nods. 'I know. That was lousy . . . to you . . . to me . . . to Betty. I wasn't being fair to anyone. Look, Marcy, I just walked her up to her cabin and then came right back down again to talk to Carl.'

'Honest?'

'Honest.'

I hug him.

He kisses me on the top of the head and then on my mouth.

When we stop, he says, 'I think we've got a volleyball game.'

'I hate volleyball,' I say. 'I like kissing better.'

'Me too,' Ted says. 'But they've challenged us to the championship.'

'Do you think we can change it to a kissing championship?' I ask and grin.

He grins back. 'They might win. I think they've got more experience.'

'We could practise a lot.'

He takes my hand, and we go over to the volleyball net. It's very dark. There were lights by the swings but not here.

Barbara and Carl are pretending to serve.

There's no ball.

Ted and I get on the other side of the net.

'Ready,' Carl yells.

'Serve,' Ted and I yell.

I pretend to hit it back.

Barbara slams 'it' down over the net. 'Our point.'

'Cheat,' I scream. 'Your hands were over the net.'

I can't really see but it doesn't matter.

We argue about that for a while and then decide to give them half a point.

We then get half a point for a disputed ball.

Another serve.

A return.

'It bounced twice,' Ted yells.

I can't believe it. It's pitch dark and we're playing volleyball without a volleyball.

Final score: 21½ to 21½.

No one loses.

We're all winners.

Game called on account of mosquitoes.

Eleven

Four days after the volleyball game and I'm in charge of bunk five.

Corrine got poison ivy.

Bad.

Her face's swollen to twice its normal size. There's a rash all over her body. She's got to wear mittens so she won't scratch.

At the infirmary right now Corrine's getting Calamine lotion poured all over her body.

I'm watching the final dress rehearsal of the skit before the talent show.

Ginger walks by.

'Hi,' I say.

She ignores me.

'What's the matter?'

'Do you care? You won't do anything about it anyway.' She looks at me.

I never did talk to Corrine. With everything else that's happened, I've been so busy, I forgot.

'Ginger. I'm sorry. How's everything going? Really. I promise we'll have a talk as soon as carnival and the talent show are over. I thought everything was going better.'

She shrugs. 'Don't bother. It's not worth it. Who cares?' and she walks away.

The girls finish up the skit and hang out in front of the cabin.

Ginger sits by herself under a tree and draws. Risa and Linda go into the cabin.

A few minutes later they start to scream.

There's a bat in bunk five.

Oh no, not again.

Corrine's in the infirmary.

No one else is around but me.

I've got to deal with it even though I'm scared.

I can do it. At least I think I can. I'm learning that things happen that aren't always wonderful, but I can handle it. It's not punishment for being good or bad, a success or a failure – it's just life. Scary, but I'll survive ... That's what I'm learning this summer, not to take everything so personally. The bat didn't wake up this morning and say, 'Oh goody, I'm going to get Marcy Lewis today.'

I can survive – and more than that, I can live my life. I've always been so afraid that I couldn't do anything on my own. Now I can do lots of things. And what I can't do, I can try to get help with.

This bat, however, is not going to help me out. It's up to me.

I thought bats only came out at night.

A bat. An ugly, vicious bat. It's probably dripping with rabies.

Linda taps me on the shoulder. 'Marcy, you've got to do something. It's flying all over the place. Our clothes are probably covered with bat turds.'

I grab a broom that someone's left on the front porch.

'Don't go,' Kitty yells.

'Don't kill it.' That's Stacey.

Everyone's upset except for Risa and Linda, who look like they're trying to keep from laughing.

It seems fishy to me.

Opening the door slowly, I look inside.

'It's in your room,' Risa yells.

Linda's rolling on the ground laughing.

I'm going to be brave.

I open the door.

On the floor of my room is a baseball bat with a sign on it: 'AUGUST FOOL!'

That's it. That's the bat in bunk five.

I pick up the bat and pretend that I'm going to clobber Linda and Risa.

I put down the bat when I realise that I really do want to clobber Risa and Linda.

Someday this is going to be very funny, but right now I'm just trying to get my heart to stop pounding so fast.

Everyone starts laughing.

Even I begin to see the humour in the situation.

There's a knock on the cabin door.

It's Carl. 'Marcy, the magazine's ready, all put together. How about you and the girls coming down to the office to put the finishing touches on it?'

'There's a bat in bunk five,' yells Risa.

Carl looks at me.

I grin. 'In my room, take a look.'

He does and comes out laughing.

I can't believe I used to be afraid of him.

We all go to the office to work on the magazine. It looks great. I'm really proud of it.

Corrine walks in and calls me over to the side. 'Marcy, I'm going to stay in the infirmary for a day or two until this clears up. I feel terrible. I can't believe it. Would you be in charge of the candy floss machine tomorrow for the carnival? Barbara says it's all right, that someone will show you how to work it. I can't. It's hard to twirl paper cones with mittens on my hands. Also I think the Board of Health would view it as a health hazard to ooze poison ivy on to candy floss.'

'Sure,' I say, seeing how bad she looks. 'Do you want me to do anything else?'

She hands me an envelope. 'Here. Katherine wrote this list for me of the stuff I need from the bunk. Would you please have one of the kids pack a suitcase for me and deliver it to the infirmary?'

I nod. 'Want me to walk you back?'

'No thanks. I just had to get out for a minute before I went stir crazy.'

She leaves, and I give Betsy the list so she can get Corrine's stuff.

Lunchtime.

It starts to rain. Oh no, the dreaded downpour. That's one of the worst things that can happen at camp, having everyone closed in for a long period of time.

Everyone remains in the main house after lunch.

One of the upstairs rooms is set up with arts and crafts supplies.

Another is turned into a rehearsal room for skits practice.

Most of the kids stay on the ground floor, running, yelling, and joking around.

Someone lets the goats in.

The campers have a great time rounding them up, pretending it's a rodeo.

Once the goats are outside again, we push aside the tables and chairs and set up a kickball game. Ted heads one team and Sally heads the other.

I referee.

The noise level's high. It sounds like a rock concert.

I hope the rain lets up soon.

Heidi comes over. She's wearing an orange hooded rain poncho with the baseball cap on top of it. 'I hope this clears up and the sun dries everything out. It'd be awful if carnival had to be postponed. The kids are really looking forward to it.'

Ted's team is up to kick and it's his turn.

I watch as he kicks and rounds the bases.

'I'm glad you two got everything straightened out,' Heidi says. Then, 'I kind of wish I'd met someone here. Oh well, I suppose I could always take Jimmy up on his offer and go look at his newspaper clippings.'

'You're kidding,' I say.

She grins. 'I'm kidding. I'd rather be alone than with someone just to be with someone. If they learn how to clone people, I'd like to have one made from Ted.'

I tell her the Bozo the Clone joke.

We laugh.

It's good to have a friend who isn't jealous because you're doing something she's not. I really like Heidi.

Finally the rain stops and we can go outside.

Back to our regular activities.

Then on to dinner. A lot of camp seems to centre around the dining room. I hope I'm not gaining weight. But I don't think so. My clothes still fit, and I'm getting lots of exercise.

Then we have a campfire, only we have to hold it inside, using the dining room fireplace because the ground's still wet from the rain.

A special treat. Hot chocolate with marshmallows. And Somemores: graham cracker sandwiches with melted marshmallows and a piece of chocolate inside. For the kids who don't want sugar, there is a special package of nuts and raisins.

Then it's off to bed.

I'm in charge and nothing's gone wrong. What a relief. I'll be glad when Corrine feels better and comes back. I miss her.

Sleep, then get up. There's definitely a pattern to camp.

Carnival's to begin just before lunch, a break in the pattern.

Twelve

The big field, next to the dining hall, is ready.

The staff are really busy.

We've set the booths up.

The sun, thank goodness, is shining.

Some of the staff are roaming around, making sure the bigger kids don't try to take the rolls of tickets away from the little kids. The tickets have been given out so that the kids can 'buy' things. Each kid gets the same amount of tickets with certain categories printed on them. That's to make sure not all of the tickets are used just for one thing – all food . . . or all games . . . or all pony rides.

The camp's really gone all out on this.

There are booths where the kids can paint

themselves with body paint. Others where they can batik cloth, do water gun painting; there's even a dunk-the-staff member booth, lots of booths.

I go over to the candy floss machine.

Ted's got the booth right next to mine – toffee apples. I think he swapped with someone to get it.

We're both wearing the T-shirts we bought in Woodstock.

'Ready?' he asks.

I nod. 'Corrine explained to me how it works. It would be just my luck to break a rented machine.'

'I'll help.' He comes over and puts his arm around my shoulder.

We look at the machine.

'Shouldn't be too hard,' I say. Since I've been at camp, I'm not so scared to try out new things.

We turn the machine on, pour sugar and food colouring in, and like magic, spun sugar starts to collect on the sides of the machine.

I grab a paper cone and twirl it around the machine.

Ted turns off the machine while we look at

the first cone of candy floss. It's lopsided, but it'll do.

Ted takes a bite out of it and then gives me a kiss.

'Sticky lips,' I say.

He grins.

Ellen comes over. 'Traitor. How can you two work at these things? Candy floss and toffee apples. I'm going to put up a sign telling kids to boycott this junk.'

We let her. I'm not sure that she's wrong, but it's going to have to be something each kid decides for himself or herself. Ted goes back to his booth.

Ellen's sign, POISON, with a skull and crossbones, doesn't seem to be stopping a lot of the kids.

They've been let loose and are all running around, with long lines at Ted's and my booths.

Alvin comes running up with his tickets. 'I want a candy floss and a toffee apple.'

'Don't forget to get a hot dog or hamburger,' I say.

'You sound like my mother,' he says. 'This is camp. Give me a break.'

I give him the candy floss and take his ticket.
There's a long line.

The candy floss is a real mess to make. How come it always looks so easy when other people make it? The stuff keeps globbing up on the sides of the machine, and I have to keep stopping and scooping all the goop off. I'm covered from head to foot with candy floss.

Ted looks my way. 'What a sweet person you are. Sugar and spice and everything nice, that's what little girls . . .'

I walk over to him and cover his face with candy floss. 'Sweets for the sweet, you male chauvinist.'

Alvin runs up, crying. He shows us his toffee apple. One of Alvin's teeth is attached to it.

I don't think it's the right time to say I told you so.

Sally runs over to me. 'Marcy. I'm here to relieve you. It's time for you to go to the dunk-the-counsellor booth.'

I look at Alvin.

'It's okay. I can take care of him,' Ted says, pulling candy floss off his face and sticking it down my back. 'Just remember that the next time you're tempted to call me a male chauvinist.'

I give them both a kiss and go take my place on the 'dunking board'.

It's set up by the pool.

I have to sit down on the diving board, fully clothed.

A target area's set up nearby. If someone throws a ball through the middle of the target, someone behind me pushes me into the water.

Kitty aims and misses. She tries again. Safe. She's got really bad aim.

So does Risa.

And Linda.

Stacey's been practising. She gets the target twice.

I'm pushed into the pool twice.

Soaking wet.

Bobbie aims and gets me.

I'm in the water again.

The water's made the mess from the candy floss even worse.

Alicia, Ginger, and Janie throw together. One ball hits me and the other hits the target.

Down and wet again.

Betsy and Robin miss.

A breather.

Some of the kids from the writing group get me.

'Isn't my time up yet?' I yell.

'Not yet. Our turn.' It's Barbara, Carl, and Ted.

'But I thought you were my friends,' I say as I go down again.

Finally my time's up and it's Ted's turn.

I get him.

I wave goodbye, go up to the bunk, change, and go back to the candy floss machine.

By the end of the afternoon I'm exhausted and it's not over yet.

The talent show. All of the bunks perform. Then the individual kids perform. Then some of the counsellors. There's a lot of talent at this place.

Then there's a campfire and everyone sings.

By the time we finally sing, 'Day is done, gone the sun', it's very late.

We help carry the little kids who've fallen asleep up to the bunks.

The kids crawl into bed.

They're exhausted too.

I do a bed check and then go to sleep.

Camp's three-quarters over.

Next weekend's Visitors' Day.

It's going too fast.

That's the last thing I remember before I fall asleep.

I'm awakened in the morning by Janie.

She hands me a piece of paper with writing on it.

It's from Ginger.

She's run away.

Thirteen

Ginger's gone.

I read her note over several times. Each time my stomach turns more.

Dear (ha!) Bunk Five,
I'm gone. Who are you going to pick on now? Nobody pays any attention to me anyway. It'll probably be the last day of camp before you even notice I'm gone. I was in your dumb skit even though no one hung out with me at the carnival or sat with me at the campfire.

I hate you all.
Ginger Simon

'Did anyone hear or see her leave?' I ask, feeling like my insides are going to erupt out of my body.

The girls crowd into my room.

No one did.

Betsy says, 'Marcy, what are we going to do?'

'I don't know. I wish Corrine was here.' I'm beginning to feel numb. 'I feel so guilty.'

'It's not your fault,' Helene says.

'It's all our faults,' Risa says.

I try to figure out what's best, even though it's hard to think. 'Someone get dressed fast and take this note to Barbara and Carl.'

'I'll do it,' Robin says, taking the note and rushing out.

I jump out of bed. 'Everyone get ready. Check out the bathroom and around the cabins. Then meet me in the dining room.'

I throw on clothes and rush to the dining room, remembering how I said I was going to help her and then pretty much ignored her.

By the time I get there, Barbara and Carl are waiting by the bell.

'I'm sorry,' I say. 'I didn't know she was this

upset. It's all my fault. I should have listened to her.'

'Let's worry about whose fault this is after we find her. When did she leave? Did she take her clothes or anything with her? Does anyone have an idea of what she could be wearing?' Carl is holding the note.

'I don't know.' I look down at the ground.

Robin offers to go back to the bunk to check out Ginger's clothes. She runs back up to the bunk.

A lot of people are arriving for breakfast.

Soon everyone knows what's happening.

Jimmy walks up 'The other day Arnie was taking Polaroid pictures by the pool. I think he's got one or two with Ginger. Maybe that'll help if we have to call the police.'

The police. Oh no. This is really serious. What if something terrible happens to her? What if she falls down and gets killed? I'd never be able to look at myself in the mirror again.

'Let's stay calm,' Barbara says. 'It won't help if we look upset. That'll only make the rest of the kids more upset.'

'I'll help search,' Jimmy says.

Maybe he's not so bad after all.

Ted comes over. 'What can I do?' He puts his arm around my waist.

I stand there thinking about all of the time I spend with Ted. I should have spent some of it with Ginger.

'We can all go inside,' Carl says.

Robin reports. Some of Ginger's clothing is gone.

Once everybody goes inside, breakfast is quickly served and the meeting begins.

'Attention,' Carl says. 'We've got to have silence in order to discuss this.'

It quietens down immediately, and Carl asks if Ginger had confided to anyone about running away.

She hadn't.

He explains that running away never solves anything because you take your problems with you.

Barbara tells everyone that the camp activities for the day will revolve around the pool and sports areas. That'll free a lot of staff members to look for Ginger. She calls out the names of the staff who will search.

My name's not on the list.

After everyone goes outside, except for the searchers who are awaiting instructions, I go up to Barbara.

'Please let me look,' I say. 'It'll make me feel better.'

She shakes her head. 'It may make you feel better, but I don't think it's what's best for the rest of the kids in the bunk, Marcy. You'll be more useful here being with them.'

I go outside, feeling awful.

Sandy, the counsellor who refused to have Ginger in her bunk, comes up to me. 'Marcy, I'm sorry this had to happen. I warned Barbara. Ginger needs more than we can give her.'

'But I thought maybe I could reach her.' I shake my head. 'But I didn't do enough, actually hardly anything. She was nasty whenever I attempted to talk to her.'

'Look, you tried. She's really manipulative. She's done just about everything to get attention. This is her latest. I only hope she gets some help before she really hurts herself.'

I stare at the ground. 'Thanks, that makes me

feel a little better. I just hope they find her and she's all right.'

I look up to check on the rest of the girls in bunk five. They're all sitting together, under a tree.

Saying goodbye to Sandy, I walk over and join them.

Kitty says, 'We should have been nicer to Ginger.'

I think about what Sandy just said. 'Maybe. But I think none of us could've given her all that she wants or needs. Don't blame yourselves.'

'She was getting a little better. She only called me a moron once in a while instead of every few minutes.' Ellen arranges rocks in a pile.

'She taught me to swim,' Janie cries.

That makes me wonder more about Ginger. She's so hard to figure out.

Alicia shakes her head. 'I hope Ginger's okay, but we've got to remember that she's done lots of bad things to us. She started it. How long do we have to turn the other cheek?'

They all start to talk at once.

'She used a lanyard stitch on the laces of my

ballet slippers,' says Betsy.

'And she licked all of my stamps so the glue's gone and they're hard to use,' Ellen says.

'What about the time she told one of the little kids that eating the bark of the tree would help him fly? That kid could've died if the counsellor hadn't pulled him out of the tree.'

'I should have listened to her when she wanted to talk,' I say.

'One of the goats should've eaten her,' Helene says.

'Look, everything will work out,' I say to reassure them. 'Now, I think it would be a good idea for all of you to take part in some activity. Okay?'

They get up and go over to the basketball court, to play 'horse'. That's the game where you've got to make the basket the way the person in front does, if the basket's made. Missing means getting a letter. If you keep missing and get all five letters, you're a 'horse' and you're out.

I sit on the sidelines, watch the game, and keep hoping Ginger will turn up.

Linda comes over and sits down.

'You out already?' I ask.

'I'm just HO, but I thought I should tell you something. Ginger once bragged she had some extra money hidden – about twenty dollars – that she didn't turn in at the canteen like she was supposed to do.'

'Are you sure?'

Linda nods. 'Yeah. She showed it to me and bragged that her father sent it to her. She kept it in her baseball mitt.'

'Please, Linda, go up and see if it's gone.'

'Okay, but you've got to take my turn at basketball.'

I nod and go over to play.

Linda rushes back in a few minutes, out of breath. 'It's gone. So's the mitt.'

'Please go tell Barbara.'

'First tell me how many letters I've got now that you took over.'

'HORS.'

As she runs off, she yells, 'Change the game to "horsie", I'll be back in a minute.'

When she returns, I gladly get out of the game.

Barbara and Corrine come over.

'I know it's too late to apologise, but I want

167

you to know Ginger did try to talk to me a while ago, but I was too involved with other stuff. And then, last morning, she was mad at me, and I don't think I handled it right.' I have to confess.

Barbara frowns. 'Marcy, I know I told you you didn't have to be perfect, but this time I wish you were. But I'm not sure that anyone could have known what the best way to handle the situation is.'

Corrine starts to scratch. 'Dumb poison ivy. I could be out there looking for her right now if . . .'

Barbara says, 'Half the camp's looking. So are the police. It's okay that you can't search.'

'Have you heard any news?' I want to know.

'Carl and Ted just called in. I told them about Ginger's twenty dollars. They're going to check out the bus stops in Woodstock and Kingston.'

'If she left here in the middle of the night, she could be long gone to anywhere,' Corrine says.

'Well, we've contacted both of her parents. Since they're divorced, she may go to either one of them. They're awaiting further word from us, and they'll let us know if she runs to them. Somehow I doubt it though. I don't think she likes either of them very much.' Barbara shakes her head. 'I don't think Ginger's had an easy home life.'

I'm so nervous. I feel as if my head's going to explode and my stomach hurts all the way to my legs. The only other time I ever felt this bad or felt so helpless was the night my father had the heart attack and the ambulance took him away.

Finally it's lunchtime. Everyone comes in for a quick meal and goes out again.

Still no word.

The crafts teachers bring down rolls of lanyard materials and hooks.

Soon a lot of the kids have put the hooks on trees and are working on the lanyards. It looks like the kids are attached to the trees. I wonder what the kids do with all the lanyards when they get home. Probably they give them to their parents as presents. I can just see an executive going to work with a lanyard and a briefcase. Maybe it'll become a new fashion fad.

Some of the searchers return to say they've had no luck.

We're in the middle of the woods. I don't know where she could have gone.

More searchers return.

The police check in.

No luck.

It's enough to drive someone crazy.

It's almost dinnertime, and they still haven't found her.

One of the goats comes up and sniffs at my sneaker. Maybe the goats can be trained as police goats, sniff an article of clothing, and find a missing person.

Finally Katherine, who's on phone duty, sends a messenger out to us.

Carl and Ted have called in.

They've found Ginger on the village green at Woodstock.

They're on the way back to camp.

Relief.

Barbara rings the bell to let everyone know.

I start to cry.

So do a few other people.

Now I know how my parents felt the time I

was five and got lost at Disney World. I want to hug Ginger. I want to kill her.

But most of all I want to understand why she did it.

Fourteen

'How about some food? I only had one slice of pizza and a soda all day.' Ginger sits on a chair in Carl and Barbara's living room.

Corrine, Carl, Barbara, and I look at each other.

Ginger continues. 'My parents paid for my meals. You owe me three.'

Barbara says, 'And you owe us an explanation.'

Ginger looks at her Woodstock purchases.

We all stare at her.

She smiles, says nothing, and continues to take things out of bags.

With the amount of money that she has obviously spent, she couldn't have been planning to take a bus anyplace. I bet she had no intention of staying away longer than for the day.

I could murder her.

Barbara looks ready to explode. 'You're very pleased with yourself, aren't you? Well, I've had it. We keep giving you chances and you keep holding out. Don't you realise what could have happened, running away? Hitch-hiking? I don't know what to do any more.'

Ginger says, 'I thought you never gave up.'

Carl takes Barbara's hand and pats it. 'Ginger, do you want to tell us why you ran away?'

'No.' She gives him a wide grin.

He shakes his head. 'I wish you would. Then we might be able to help you.'

I want Ginger to talk, to explain. It's so hard to understand her.

'Your parents have been called and are on their way up,' Barbara tells her.

For the first time Ginger's not smiling. 'No. I don't want to see them.'

'They're on their way up,' Barbara repeats.

'No.' Now Ginger's yelling. 'I don't want to see them. Call them back and tell them not to come.'

'We've got to have a conference with them,' Carl says.

Ginger stands up and tries to run out of the room.

Carl stops her.

She kicks him and tries to get away.

He holds on to her.

She kicks and screams for a while and then goes limp and sobs.

Carl lifts her up and sits down on the chair, holding her.

Barbara goes over, stoops down, and strokes her hair.

Ginger continues to sob.

The tears start to stream down my face. I'm not even sure why I'm crying.

Corrine's staring at her mittens, her face still swollen with poison ivy.

No one says anything for a few minutes.

Finally Ginger looks up. 'Please don't make me go home with one of my parents. Let me stay.'

Carl says, 'I don't think we can help you enough.'

Ginger looks at me. 'It's Marcy's fault. I

wanted to talk to her, and she didn't have time.'

I feel as though I've been shot through my heart.

Everyone looks at me.

'You should send her home too,' Ginger says. 'If I have to go, so should she.'

I panic. Maybe they will send me home. Maybe I should be sent home. I'm probably the worst counsellor-in-training ever.

Barbara shakes her head. 'Ginger, you're still trying to run things your way, blaming everyone else. Marcy's not the only person to talk to, and anyway, I know that she did try to talk to you in the beginning, and you made it impossible.'

'She likes everyone else better than me. So does Corrine. So do you. So does everyone.' Ginger starts to rock back and forth in Carl's arms.

Carl shakes his head. 'You can't treat people the way that you do and expect them to take it.'

Ginger continues to cry. 'I'll apologise to everyone, tell them I'm sorry. Corrine, I'm sorry that I rubbed wet poison ivy all over your sheets. I won't do it again.'

I look at Corrine.

She looks like she could kill Ginger.

Barbara gets up. 'I think Corrine and Marcy should go now.'

The three of us walk outside.

'I'd strangle that monster if I weren't wearing mittens,' Corrine says. 'I really hate her.'

'She is rather hard to love,' Barbara says. 'I don't know what to do any more. I really thought that I could help her, but she's too much for me. I'm going to recommend that her parents get professional help for her.'

I think of the counselling that my family got and hope that it works for Ginger too.

I used to think that things were the worst in my family. Now I can really see that other people have problems too.

We all stand in front of the house for a few minutes, saying nothing.

Finally I speak. The suspense is killing me. 'Are you going to send me home too?'

Corrine says, 'Please don't. Marcy's a really good CIT.'

'I know that.' Barbara looks at us. 'Who died and left Ginger in charge?'

'I was going to try to reach her,' I confess.

'Then I got all tied up with other things.'

'I know.' Barbara nods. 'Part of camp is your own growth and experience. I'm not sure that any of us are aware of what Ginger's going through. Look, I'd better go back inside and make sure that she and Carl are doing all right.'

She returns to her house.

Corrine says, 'I'm going back to the infirmary for more Calamine lotion. You'd better go back to the bunk.'

I nod and start to go up the hill.

'Marcy.' Corrine runs up to me. 'I just want you to know that I think you've done a good job but I also want you to think about how much time you've put into getting your own head together and your relationship with Ted and how much time you've spent getting to really know the kids.'

'Do you think I've been bad?' I ask.

She shakes her head and smiles. 'Not bad. Human. You've really got to stop seeing things as all bad or all good. And you've got to learn that just because someone tells you something that you don't want to hear, doesn't mean that person's out to get you.'

I nod. My mother tells me that all the time, especially when I'm angry at something my father's said. Somehow it's different when you hear it from a friend, not a parent.

She says, 'We're still friends, right?'

I nod again. 'We could even become blood sisters, like the kids did the other day.'

'Not till I get rid of this poison ivy. That's all we'd need, to get it into cuts.' Corrine smiles.

We wave goodbye.

I think of Ted. I really want to see him, talk to him, have us hold each other.

I also want to see the kids in the bunk, find out how they're doing.

I finally understand what my parents mean when they say that there aren't enough hours in the day. I used to get so jealous when they wanted to spend some time alone together and I wanted to be with them. I think that a day should be at least thirty-five hours long.

I'm beginning to realise that it's like my glasses have been focused inwards on me and not outwards to see the rest of the people in the world. I wonder if my eye doctor can help make me a special pair of glasses so that I can see the right amount inside and outside.

I decide to go back to the cabin and see Ted later. That's what I was hired to do, to be with the kids. I knew when I signed up that it wasn't a nine-to-five job.

There's laughter coming from the bunk.

As I walk in, Linda says, 'Marcy, how many counsellors does it take to change a light bulb?'

I sigh, 'How many?'

'Only one, but the light bulb really has to want to change.'

I laugh.

Ginger. The joke makes me think of her. Maybe that's why Linda told me the joke.

Heidi's with the kids. 'If everyone in the United States owns a pink automobile, what would the country be called?'

'A pink carnation.'

Groans.

Risa yells, 'What's green and hangs from trees?'

No one knows.

She yells again. 'Giraffe snot.'

People throw pillows at her.

Finally it quietens down.

'So what's happening with Ginger?' Helene asks.

Everyone's staring at me.

'Her parents are coming up to discuss things.'

'I hope that they take her home,' Betsy says.

Alicia nods. 'They'll probably get into another fight like the one they had Visitors' Day.'

I remember. Everyone's parents came up and were standing around talking when Mrs Simon yelled at Mr Simon for not sending child-support cheques. It was absolutely awful.

'I bet neither of them wants to take her home.' Alicia makes a face.

Heidi shakes her head. 'I know it's been difficult to have Ginger in the bunk, but I think you've all learned something from this.'

'Yeah, what a creep she is.' That's from Ellen.

Heidi shakes her head. 'No, that it's not always easy to get along with everyone but that you should try to understand his or her problems.'

'You sound like Barbara,' Stacey says.

'That's not a bad thing.' I come to her defence. 'She only wants what's best for all of us. She doesn't have to be perfect.'

'That's what my parents always say when I complain about something. That they are doing their best. But that doesn't stop them from being pains,' Janie says.

'Well, they may be pains, but I think you should try to see them as human beings,' I say and think of what my parents' reaction would be if they could hear me say that. They'd probably have me write it down, sign it, and get it legalised.

Heidi says, 'My parents are always saying, "How much longer must we be punished for the things we did that we thought were right?" Maybe we should all swap parents for a while and see if it's any different.'

The girls talk about that for a while. They decide to write to their parents and tell them about how when camp's over, everyone in bunk five's going home with a different family.

'Are you serious?' I ask.

'No,' Risa says. 'You're so gullible.'

'I kind of thought it would be a good idea.' Janie smiles.

'Who should I ask to the Sadie Hawkins' Dance? That's more important right now,' Linda says. 'I don't want to go with Howard any more.'

I didn't even know that she was going with Howard. That must have been the shortest 'going together' in the world.

It's kind of hard to know who's going with whom. At camp all of the kids past a certain age seem to pair up. 'Going out' means walking together to meals and sitting together at campfires.

The girls all discuss their choices.

With summer almost over they've really changed, become a group, developed more of their individual personalities. I think that camp's a place to try out new behaviour, see what works, discover who you are in relation to other people. And that is, I'm learning, not just true for campers. It's also true for counsellors. And directors. For everyone.

I'm not sure what's going to happen to Ginger.

Or with Ted and me once camp's over.

Or with my parents when I return home feeling as different as I do.

It's really strange. I don't want camp to ever end and yet I can't wait until I get home to experience new things. It's all kind of funny and sad and joyful and exciting at the same time.

It's kind of like what I've always thought, that my life goes on like a novel with lots of character development. But there is a change. There is a plot.

I can hardly wait for the next chapter.

A NOTE FROM THE AUTHOR

The school year was 1977–1978 and I was teaching eighth and ninth graders. Many of my students had come back from summer vacation talking about their experiences at camp.

Camp. It's the time when kids leave home, meet new people, try out new behaviour.

That gave me an idea. Ever since THE CAT ATE MY GYMSUIT was published in 1974, people had been asking me to write a sequel. What if I sent Marcy to camp?

The only problem was that my only experience at camp had been a disaster. (One week after I got there, my mother became camp nurse and brought along my little brother. So much for getting away!)

Help came at the laundromat when I noticed some people washing huge amounts of towels and clothes. I saw from their sweatshirts that they were from Mt Tremper Lutheran Camp. Camp!!!!! Life was good! They invited me to visit, to take notes, to talk with campers and counsellors.

The sequel got written.

CAT. BAT. People said that I should write a third book about Marcy and have her grow up and join the RAT race. I don't think so!

I'm happy with the two books about Marcy . . . and happy that new generations of readers continue to meet her and go to camp with her.

– Paula Danziger

THE DIVORCE EXPRESS

Paula Danziger

No one wants to ride the divorce express. Especially not Phoebe. It means she has to leave her New York City apartment and her boyfriend every Sunday night to spend the week in the country with her dad. It means she has to start a new school, make new friends and watch her father go on dates. Now neither place feels like home. And then her mother makes an announcement. Can Phoebe cope with any more changes?

IT'S AN AARDVARK-EAT-TURTLE WORLD
The sequel to *The Divorce Express*

Paula Danziger

Rosie's parents divorced shortly after she was born. She's been used to being just her and her mum for years. But now her mother and her best friend's father have fallen in love and are moving in together. It seems like the perfect plan. She and her best friend, Phoebe, are delighted. At first.

But it's not so easy being part of a family again – and living with your best friend isn't all it's cracked up to be . . .

THE PISTACHIO PRESCRIPTION

Paula Danziger

Cassie Stephens is thirteen, mousey and asthmatic. She's fed up with having to look after her little brother, being teased by her older sister, and ignored by her parents, who don't seem to stop rowing.

The only thing that helps her to survive is her addiction to pistachio nuts – somehow they always make her feel better. But as the pressures of home and school mount, even the pistachio nuts don't seem to help . . .